"I think it's time [...] around," Adam said

Jane nodded, leaning against one of the metal filing cabinets that clearly had seen better days. "Sure. I'll give you the nickel tour.... Sorry we're short on the kind of fancy stuff you must be used to."

But she didn't look sorry, Adam saw. No, she seemed more amused than anything, as if she was waiting with considerable relish for him to avow needing state-of-the-art technology. Rather than give her the satisfaction, he decided it was time to wipe off that faint smirk.

"What I'm used to doesn't matter," he replied bluntly. "What counts is whether I'll agree to try and pull off a miracle by making this place profitable."

Her lips, as free of makeup as the rest of her face, thinned in a flash. "Will you?"

Despite the tension between them as they traded glances, he kept his expression bland. "I don't know yet. We still haven't finished the nickel tour...."

HUSBAND IN HARMONY
Sharon Swan

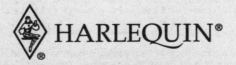

HARLEQUIN®

TORONTO • NEW YORK • LONDON
AMSTERDAM • PARIS • SYDNEY • HAMBURG
STOCKHOLM • ATHENS • TOKYO • MILAN • MADRID
PRAGUE • WARSAW • BUDAPEST • AUCKLAND

For the Phoenix Desert Rose and Valley of the Sun chapters of RWA and their group of great writers, with many thanks for the terrific support

ISBN 0-373-75019-6

HUSBAND IN HARMONY

ABOUT THE AUTHOR

Born and raised in Chicago, Sharon Swan once dreamed of dancing for a living. Instead, she surrendered to life's more practical aspects, settled for an office job and concentrated on typing and being a big Chicago Bears fan. Sharon never seriously considered writing as a career until she moved to the Phoenix area and met Pierce Brosnan at a local shopping mall. The chance meeting changed her life, because she found herself thinking *what if?* What if two fictional characters had met the same way? That formed the basis for her first story, and she's now cheerfully addicted to writing contemporary romance and playing *what if?*

Sharon loves to hear from readers. You can write her at P.O. Box 21324, Mesa, AZ 85277.

Books by Sharon Swan

HARLEQUIN AMERICAN ROMANCE

912—COWBOYS AND CRADLES
928—HOME-GROWN HUSBAND
939—HUSBANDS, HUSBANDS...EVERYWHERE!*
966—FOUR-KARAT FIANCÉE
983—HER NECESSARY HUSBAND*

*Welcome to Harmony

Chapter One

Adam Lassiter's frown came fast and hard when he got his first good look at Glory Ridge Resort and Campground in the bright light of an Arizona summer day.

"Do you mean to tell me," he said to the woman standing beside him, "that people actually pay to stay at this place?"

Jane Pitt stiffened, both at the words and the dry-as-dust tone, but managed not to answer in the same vein. She knew that giving as good as she got—normally her first response to any sort of confrontation—wouldn't serve her best interests at the moment. However she might privately feel about slick business consultants who probably thought that slaving in a ritzy office was real work, she could put up with one if she had to.

And this one was slick as spit.

Fancy gray suit, fancy red tie, fancy black leather wing tips. Every long, lean inch of him shouted *pricey.*

"No one has paid to stay here lately," Jane said with total honesty. She shoved her hands into the pockets of well-worn jeans and flicked her wheat-colored bangs aside with a shake of her head, reminding herself it was time to get the scissors out and whack some off. "That's why I'm open to advice for changing the situation."

"Free advice," her companion pointed out in his low baritone voice. He gazed down at her with steely gray eyes, and for the umpteenth time in her life Jane wished she were taller. At five feet four and not much more than a hundred pounds dripping wet, looking as formidable as she would have liked was hard. But attitude could make a difference. She'd found that out early on.

"In exchange for a free stay at one of the cabins," she countered. "I don't want something for nothing." She might not be big, but she had lots of pride.

His expression turned wary as he aimed another look at the small log cabins set against towering pines now rustled by a warm breeze. "Are there any safe enough to stay in? I'd hate to hear a roof collapsing on me in the middle of the night."

"The roofs are sound." She wouldn't mention the leaks. "The whole place just needs some fixing up."

"I'll say." He blew out a breath and ran a long-fingered hand through his dark, expertly cut hair. "From what I've seen, the best thing you've got going for you is the view."

Jane switched around to take in a scene that would impress the most jaded of people. Low mountains encircled the small, sun-splashed city of Harmony, located a hundred winding miles northeast of Phoenix and its lower desert regions. Glory Ridge ran along the side of one of those mountains. The resort named after the ridge became part of the picture back when Harmony was a much younger version of itself.

"I grew up there, you know," the man at her side said matter-of-factly.

"In Harmony?" Jane faced him again. "I figured you might have when the top guy at Hayward Investments recommended you. He said you were his cousin." In fact, Ross Hayward, who she'd been told by people in the know was good for some guidance, had suggested that Adam Lassiter's talents were just what she needed. She had to hope it was so.

"I grew up on a small ranch on the other side of this mountain," she offered by way of information.

He nodded. "So you're a native of the area, too. Hmm. I can't say that I remember the name Pitt."

"Probably because my family didn't get into town much," she allowed. She could have added that her father, with his gruff-as-a-bear nature, had never been eager to spend time in a city that prided itself on its friendliness. "I was homeschooled until my mother died after a short illness. By then, I was fourteen and ready for Harmony High."

"You don't appear to be much more than fourteen now," he stated, casting a critical eye over her.

Jane stiffened again in an automatic reaction. "I'm double that, Mr. Lassiter."

If he heard the irritation underscoring that statement, he ignored it. "My own family moved to the Phoenix area when I was still a kid," he told her. "I'm thirty-four now—and it's Adam."

She couldn't even imagine him as a boy. The man he'd become was far too self-assured.

"I go by just plain Jane," she said, well aware that truer words had never been spoken. She was plain down to her toes, something her late father had pointed out on a regular basis. At the moment, she could hardly deny that Adam Lassiter, with all his polish, made her feel even plainer. Well, to heck with it, Jane thought. She was what she was.

Adam caught the swift squaring of slender shoulders covered by a checked cotton shirt. He knew the woman he viewed was a long way from thrilled with him—had known it almost from the minute he'd pulled into the parking lot a short distance from the largest cabin in the group, which seemed to serve as the resort's headquarters. After one clearly unimpressed glance at his low-slung sports car, her hazel eyes had fixed on him as she'd walked over to introduce herself, stray strands of her short hair ruffling in the wind. And what he'd seen in her gaze could hardly be called approval.

Not that he should care one way or the other. And not that he'd even be here if he didn't have his own agenda. Whether he decided to take Jane Pitt up on her offer would depend on how much it suited his goals as well as hers.

"I think it's time for a better look around," he said.

She nodded. "Sure, I'll give you the nickel tour."

Which was all a tour might wind up being worth, Adam reflected. He had to admit that he'd been thrown off balance by what he'd seen so far. For all the beauty of the surrounding area, no one with eyes could deny that the resort was in sad shape—a lot sadder shape than he'd bargained on. "Should we start here?" he asked, keeping his tone mild as he indicated the larger cabin with a slant of his head. "I assume that's where the office is."

"Right." Jane led the way down a short gravel path, then up a step and across a narrow covered porch. She tugged open an old screen door and stepped inside.

Adam followed her into a room bordered by thick log walls and saw mostly what he'd expected to see. The scene gave, he thought, a whole new meaning to the phrase *no frills*. Nothing had probably been altered much from the time the place was first built. A long counter, the green tiles topping it scarred with age, stood at one side of the room and an ancient refrigerator at the other.

Jane glanced over at him. "Want a can of cold pop?"

He would have preferred bottled water, but he only nodded. Something told him you took what you could get with this woman. "I can help myself," he said.

For the first time, she smiled a faint smile, showing a hint of small white teeth. "Good. I like a man who doesn't expect to be waited on."

Adam let that comment hang and started for the refrigerator. When he opened it he found several varieties of soda sharing space with two large coffee cans. "Looks as though someone has a caffeine habit."

"I like it as well as the next person," Jane said, "but one of those cans happens to be home to some worms."

Adam resisted the urge to grimace—he had a hunch that would please her far too much. Instead, he calmly chose a can of cola and closed the refrigerator.

"Ever been worm hunting…Adam?" she asked, using his given name for the first time.

"Not lately…Jane," he replied, and popped the

can open. He didn't miss the amused glint in her eye as he took a long swallow. Okay, so he hadn't gone digging for fish bait since he was a kid, and even then he hadn't done it that often. If he wanted to be candid, he could tell her that he wasn't much of an outdoorsman—not the kind who would find this type of setting familiar, at any rate. But why admit it? If he decided to stay here, she'd probably discover it soon enough.

He glanced toward another doorway. "Is that the office?"

"Uh-huh." She started past him, her low brown boots scraping on the slatted wood floor. "Next stop on the tour."

Now he did grimace. The office was a far cry from the spacious suite he shared with a tax specialist and an investment counselor on the upper floor of a chrome and glass building in downtown Phoenix. Here, modern efficiency obviously didn't rule. In fact, it was nowhere in sight.

Both the small pine desk and tall metal filing cabinets had seen better days. Two chairs and a short table holding an empty coffeemaker—all of which might be judged antiques by some and junk by others—completed the furnishings. In the stark light streaming in through a bare window, everything appeared so much a part of the past that the contemporary phone and answering machine combination resting on the desk seemed out of place. The best thing he would say about the room was that it, like the outer room, was clean. Working up a shine would be hard, but dirt and dust had clearly been dealt with.

"Sorry we're short on the kind of fancy stuff you

must be used to,'' Jane said as she leaned a shoulder against one of the cabinets.

But she didn't look sorry, Adam saw with a sidelong glance. No, she still seemed more amused than anything, as if she were waiting with considerable relish for him to avow needing state-of-the-art technology. Rather than giving her that satisfaction, he decided it was time to wipe off that faint smirk.

"What I'm used to doesn't matter," he replied bluntly, turning to meet her eyes. "What counts is whether I'll agree to try and pull off a miracle by making this place profitable."

Her lips, as free of any makeup as the rest of her face, thinned in a flash. "Will you?"

Despite the thick tension between them as they traded stares, he kept his gaze bland. "I don't know yet. We still haven't finished the nickel tour."

SHE STARTED the next leg of the tour with the word *miracle* still ringing in her mind. Was that what she expected Adam Lassiter to pull off? He'd just said so in no uncertain terms, and maybe he was right, Jane had to concede, even though his candor had spiked her blood pressure.

After all, she'd known from the day she'd become determined to put the resort back on the map that it wouldn't be easy. But that didn't mean she intended to give up. Not hardly.

"How did you wind up the owner of this place?" Adam asked as they strolled toward the weathered log cabin closest to the office. Like its fellow cabins, it had a name. The rough wooden sign over the narrow front doorway declared this one to be Squirrel Hollow.

"My great-aunt left it to me when she passed away this spring," Jane explained.

He slid her a probing sidelong glance. Apparently, he caught at least a trace of sadness in her calm expression, one born of the recent loss of someone she'd both admired and been so fond of, because he said, "I'm sorry."

Jane climbed two short steps up to a narrow porch that held a spindled rocker dulled by age. "Thanks," she told him. "I appreciate the thought. Although," she added with typical frankness, "I have to admit that Maude Pitt would be the last person to invite anyone to mourn her. She'd say that she lived a good life doing exactly what she wanted to do. Which was run this place as she saw fit without wasting time taking orders from the male half of the population."

"Hmm." Adam slid another glance her way. This time it was one more rueful than probing. "Why am I thinking that you take after her?"

A wry smile tugged at her lips. "Because I just might in some ways, I suppose. I started helping out around here when I was still a child. Even though she was hardly the motherly type—she'd never had much desire to marry and raise a bunch of kids—Maude taught me a lot." *And provided a refuge from a family situation by no means always happy,* Jane reflected.

What would she have done had she not been able to ride her bike over the mountain and Maude and Mother Nature had not taken her to another, far less quarrelsome, world? Jane didn't have an answer for that question. She could only be grateful that Glory Ridge Resort and Campground had been there for her at a time when she'd needed it most.

It hadn't taken her long as a young girl to fall in love with the place, that was for sure. And she still loved it, even though it had only continued to slide downhill during her aunt's declining years.

That was why she was willing to deal with slick consultants—even one who might be the slickest of the bunch.

"This cabin will give you an idea of what the rest are like," Jane said, opening the screen door, then the simple wood door behind it. She didn't say that this was the best of the lot, although it was. It had two bedrooms. And no leaks in the roof. At least, she'd seen no signs of any.

Adam didn't hesitate to investigate, checking out the small living room with adjoining kitchen and even smaller bedrooms—themselves large compared with the tiny bath.

"So it doesn't get any better than this," he said at last with a gusty sigh, clearly intimating that the cabin had seen few changes during the past several decades.

"That's right," she replied.

In fact, it got worse. Many of the cabins, including the one she occupied a stone's throw away, had a single bedroom and a roof sporting at least a few holes. Still, the place she called home these days suited her, leaks and all. Like her great-aunt before her, she happily traded the comforts many considered a part of everyday living for the chance to experience another sort of life entirely. But this man...

"If you decide to stay," she told Adam, "you can have this cabin. It's not the Ritz—"

"You can say that again," he muttered.

"But," she said, forging on, "it has hot water,

thanks to an electric water heater, and the stove, refrigerator and all the lights around the place work fine.''

She didn't bother to point out that the appliances were downsized versions, a necessity rather than a choice with space at a premium; or that the overhead light fixtures and scattered lamps were a lot more functional than fancy. Not to mention that the rest of the cabin's furnishings, including the sturdy pine living-room chairs with the faded plaid cushions, could be termed "old-fashioned rustic"—a definite emphasis on *old*. But Adam Lassiter had taken note of all of that, she recognized, though he started for the porch without saying as much. Or saying anything.

Once they were outside again, Jane resumed her role of tour guide with dogged determination. "Quail Lake is this way," she said, and began to stride down a winding path through the trees. "A creek that feeds into it circles through the middle of the resort before it ends at the lake," she explained. Moments later they came to an arched wooden bridge just wide enough to allow two people to cross side by side.

"I assume this is the creek, even though it doesn't seem to be feeding water into anything at the moment," Adam said, looking over a short, slatted railing at a hollowed-out patch of rocky ground.

"That's why it's called Dry Creek," she told him. "It's only wet when it rains enough higher up in the mountains to fill it with some of the run off. Then it can hold anywhere from a trickle to several feet of water. I even recall Aunt Maude saying that it overflowed its banks once."

More cabins lined the path on the other side of the bridge. "Jackrabbit Junction," Adam murmured, reading the sign on the first cabin they came to. Behind it, another was barely visible at the top of a small hill. "What's that one called?" he asked.

"Eagle's Nest." Jane matched her stride to his, something she had to work at since her legs were nowhere near as long as Adam Lassiter's.

"I suppose that fits," he allowed.

The last cabin on the tour was Angler's Lair, located only yards from Quail Lake. A bird whistled high overhead as Jane led the way down to her favorite spot at Glory Ridge, and in a matter of moments they were standing close enough to hear the gentle slap of water against a winding, grassy shore.

"Well, this is another plus for the place," Adam acknowledged as he stared out at the deep blue lake sparkling in the sunshine.

He hadn't spared more than a glance at the rickety dock and the old rowboats tied there, some with outboard motors. No, right now the quiet lake, looking much as it probably had when the first settlers arrived, drew his attention, as it always drew hers.

"Quail Lake is a long way from being the biggest body of water in the region," she said, "but it's got to be the most beautiful."

"You could be right," he told her. "Is it part of the resort property?"

"Yes. The fact that the lake is privately owned has always been a plus, because fishermen don't have to invest in a license to try their luck here."

"Still, a lot of them have decided to try their luck elsewhere," he said, shifting his gaze from the lake to her. *And who could blame them?* an ironic slant of his chiseled mouth seemed to add.

Refusing to bristle again, Jane opted for the simple

truth. "Several other resorts targeting not only the fishing crowd but hikers and other outdoor types have opened in the area during the past several years, and since their facilities are newer, it's taken its toll."

He lifted a hand and ran it through his hair. "But you still want to make a go of this place."

Although it was a statement rather than a question, Jane answered. "I do. I have some of Aunt Maude's life insurance money left, plus what I've managed to save by taking whatever work I could find in Harmony, in addition to working here. It's a considerable sum—or it is to me."

Because tiptoeing around any subject had seldom been her style, Jane went on to disclose her current balance at the town's largest bank. It was probably nowhere near a successful consultant's bank account. Nevertheless, it had one of Adam's eyebrows lifting.

"I guess you know how to save money," he said.

She dipped her head in a brisk nod. "I don't usually spend much on myself."

For an instant, his eyes raked her from head to toe. She could all but hear him thinking, *That's obvious.* However, he said only, "Well, it's definitely enough to give you a good start on making some changes around here."

Changes Jane was ready to make. Finally. Maude, for all her talent at plain talk, had put off discussing any improvements, even though her great-niece had pressed her more than once. The delay had served no purpose but to send still more outdoorsmen off to other places to spend their money. It was time—past time, Jane knew—to act.

"What I need now is some savvy advice on what

changes would appeal to the most customers," she said. Her gaze met Adam's. "Will you take me up on my offer?"

He studied her for a long moment. "I just might...provided you can meet my conditions. One, actually."

A condition? That was the first she'd heard of anything along those lines. "And what would that be?" Jane asked carefully.

"If I decide to act as your consultant, I want to bring my son with me when I come back to stay here."

She was surprised and knew it showed. Somehow, she hadn't imagined this man with children. Or a wife, for that matter. Despite telling herself on first seeing him that she wasn't interested one way or the other, she'd noticed that he wore no wedding ring. He'd probably noticed the same thing about her— and not that he cared, either.

Jane arched a brow. "How, uh, old is your son?"

"Eight. His name is Sam." Adam shoved his hands into the pockets of his crisply pressed trousers. "Although I share custody with my ex-wife, Sam stays with her most of the year and spends his summers with me. After Ariel and I divorced a few years ago, she moved back to Boston, where she grew up."

He had—or used to have—a wife named *Ariel?* Talk about fancy, Jane thought. Then again, it only made sense that this man would have chosen a far-from-average woman as his bride. "How did your son wind up being called Sam?" she had to ask. Bestowing such a simple name seemed out of character for parents who were hardly ordinary.

"Actually, it's Samuel Lawrence, after both his grandfathers," Adam explained.

"I see." She paused. "Is he here in Arizona now?"

Adam nodded. "He's spending the day with my folks, who live in Scottsdale."

Oh, right. Jane did a mental eye roll. Of course his parents would live in Scottsdale, one of the ritziest sections of Phoenix. She'd never been to Scottsdale. Or anywhere else, she had to admit. But that didn't mean she was pining to see the world. She truly wasn't. She was content—more than content— where she was.

"I suppose," she allowed, "if a boy likes the outdoors, he might enjoy spending a summer in the mountains."

"Sam was raised in the city, as I was," Adam said after the briefest of hesitations. With that, he looked back out at the lake and let the subject drop.

Jane frowned. To her, his short statement only brought up more questions. One major question, at any rate: why was he set on bringing his city-raised son to a place the boy might not even like? Although this time she won the battle with her curiosity and didn't ask, something told her that there was more to the matter.

"Well, you're welcome to have him come with you," she said, "if you decide to stay here."

Adam ran his tongue over his teeth, realizing it was time to make up his mind. If he didn't have his own agenda to consider, he might tell Jane Pitt thanks but no thanks. For all that he'd been raised in a well-to-do family, he'd never been leery of working hard and tackling a challenge in the process. In fact, he had worked damn hard to get where he was in the business world.

Nevertheless, while his bid for success had paid off for himself and his clients, the blunt fact of the matter was that Glory Ridge Resort just might prove to be the exception. Despite his past track record and the substantial money the current owner was ready to invest, could the place ever be counted on to turn a consistent profit given the increased competition she'd indicated had sprung up in the area?

It would take more than money, he suspected. If he was right, it would take an idea, a pitch, a twist on the usual, to grab the public's attention and draw people to this place. Hell, maybe it *would* take a miracle.

Whatever the case, since he had his own reasons for spending some time in a quiet, out-of-the-way spot—and he couldn't think of a quieter, more out-of-the-way spot than this pine-strewn mountain—he felt compelled to give helping Jane Pitt with her objectives a try.

"Okay, I'll take you up on your offer." He turned his head and dropped his gaze to look straight at the woman beside him. "I'll be back the day after tomorrow, with my son."

She stared up at him, her calm expression betraying little of her feelings at that news. "Good," she said after a moment. "I'll get your cabin ready for you."

He'd be living in a cabin called Squirrel Hollow. Adam suppressed a wince at the thought that it was probably as far from his upscale modern condo in Phoenix as he would ever get. "I don't imagine it has a telephone hookup," he said as they started back the way they'd come, feet crunching on the gravel path.

"Nope. Only phone line is at the office, but as the crow flies we're near enough to Harmony for cell phones to work. I assume you've got one."

"Yes." He didn't go on to say that he also had all his important contact information programmed into his Palm Pilot. No matter where he was, he could generally reach his clients and business associates with little trouble. "I was thinking more of a place to hook up my laptop," he explained. "I'll need to do some research online while I'm here. I guess I'll have to tie up the office line to get it done."

She lifted one shoulder in a shrug. "Well, it's not as if people are phoning nonstop to make reservations." Her mouth drooped at one corner. "I just have to hope the situation changes down the road."

"I intend to do my best to accomplish that," Adam said, and meant it.

"Looks as if we're about to join forces," she replied in a voice that held more than its share of irony, as though she were reflecting on the fact that they made one odd couple indeed.

He could hardly deny it. The truth was, he'd never met a woman quite like Jane Pitt. He knew he ruffled her feathers, just as he knew she'd come to the conclusion that she needed his help in spite of it. They said that politics made strange bedfellows, but so did other situations.

Not that he was planning on luring Jane Pitt into his bed. Even though he hadn't taken advantage of the comforts only a willing female could provide in a while, he'd have to be a lot dumber than he was to make a move on Jane. Handling a woman as prickly as she was, even on a business basis, would take some doing. On a private basis, a man who attempted a false step with her could wind up getting his head wrenched off and handed back to him for his trouble. Jane Pitt might be on the small side, but she'd pack a wallop when she wanted to. After less than an hour's acquaintance, he was sure on that score.

"I'll call you tomorrow and let you know what time I'll be here," he told her minutes later on reaching the spot outside the resort's office where they'd first met.

"All right." Again her calm expression revealed little. "Have a good drive back."

He started to extend his right arm for the handshake they'd foregone on his arrival. Then he stilled completely as he caught sight of an animal ambling out from between two trees. He might not be an avid outdoorsman, but he knew what it was. And that knowledge had his breath catching in his throat.

"Don't move," he said in a rough whisper.

"Why?" Jane asked, and then turned her head to follow his gaze. "Oh, it's only Sweet Pea."

"It's a *skunk,* for Pete's sake." And it was coming closer as he watched, strolling along as though it had plenty of time to get where it was going.

"A full-grown female skunk, as it happens," Jane said mildly. "Don't worry. She's by and large harmless. My great-aunt found that out when she stumbled across her one day and didn't get sprayed. Apparently, Sweet Pea started life as a domesticated animal. At least, that was the vet's opinion, since she'd been descented and neutered before she somehow wound up here. Anyway, she settled right in and became more or less a pet.''

A pet skunk. Jeez, it was time to leave. Adam whipped around and started for his car. He got in, snapped the gleaming door shut and pulled out with a final wave. His last sight of Jane Pitt was in the rearview mirror as she watched him depart, her slender hands planted on her hips. He'd soon be back, he thought, negotiating a narrow mountain road. And heaven only knows what he'd have to deal with then.

''I MANAGED TO WAIT until he was out of sight before I started hooting,'' Jane confided to her companions the following day. ''Sweet Pea had Adam Lassiter moving his long legs toward his sleek sports car at a fast clip, let me tell you.'' The memory had her grinning widely.

Jane's younger sister, Ellen, who'd always been the pretty one in the Pitt family, met her sibling's eyes in the long mirror stretched across one wall of the Cuts 'N Curls beauty salon. ''Are you sure he'll be back?'' she asked, her lips curving with clear amusement.

''Yeah, he'll be back.'' Folding her arms over the front of her well-washed white T-shirt, Jane propped one denim-clad hip against the round work island holding her sister's tools of the trade. ''He called this morning and said he and his son should get to Glory Ridge shortly after lunch tomorrow.''

''I remember Adam Lassiter as a boy,'' Ellen's current client offered from her seat in a high chrome swivel chair.

Neither Ellen nor Jane expressed any surprise at that news. Unlike many people born and raised in the area, the sisters had never been members of Hester Goodbody's first grade class at the biggest of Harmony's elementary schools. Nevertheless, it was far from a secret that the now-retired teacher recalled her past students with a memory still sharp at the advanced age of eighty-plus.

"What kind of boy was he, Miss Hester?" Jane's curiosity had her asking. She'd used both the courteous title and the respectful tone most people summoned when talking to this woman.

"A charmer," Miss Hester didn't hesitate to reply. "But intelligent, as well. I'm hardly amazed that he went on to achieve success."

Jane couldn't honestly say she'd seen the charm. But the intelligence? Yes, she had no doubt that her new consultant was smart and shrewd. "We'll see if he can put all that brainpower to good advantage and come up with something that will help the resort."

Miss Hester's blue eyes, framed by gold-rimmed glasses, sparkled with good-natured humor. "It should be interesting to see how you two get along."

Ellen gave her customer's wispy silver hair a final pat. "We're done," she said, removing a cream-colored cloth cape that fit right in with the peach and cream décor chosen by the salon's original owner. Although the shop hadn't been around as long as a few of the oldest businesses in downtown Harmony, it had nonetheless occupied its prime location on Main Street for some time.

Miss Hester viewed her reflection in the mirror. "A wonderful job, as always," she told Ellen. The petite woman, who was inches shorter than even Jane's slight height, hopped nimbly off the chair.

"Best of luck on your project," she added to Jane

before following Ellen to the front desk to pay her bill.

Jane's nose wrinkled at the smell of the permanent-wave solution another operator was using on a customer farther down the room. The long-ago summer she herself had earned extra money as a shampoo girl in this very place had been pure torture, Jane recalled. Her sister, on the other hand, was at home here, pursuing a career she was both good at and genuinely enjoyed.

"You messed with your bangs again, didn't you?" Ellen accused as she returned, sliding tip money into a pocket of her bright peach smock. A frown of exasperation marred a smooth forehead topped by a shiny crown of frosted blond curls.

"I whacked a little off last night," Jane admitted. She glanced at her handiwork in the mirror. "They don't look too bad."

Ellen's sigh was long and heartfelt. "They're crooked."

Jane shrugged. "They're out of my eyes, and that's what counts."

Shaking her head, Ellen said, "Why do I even bother caring?"

"Because you love me," Jane replied with a smile, sure of her words. She had no doubt that she'd loved, and been truly loved by, three women in her life: her gentle mother, her straight-talking great-aunt and her only sister. She'd lost two of those women, but Ellen, who now had a husband and a growing son, could still be counted on to care—always.

Confirming it, Ellen dipped her chin in a quick nod. "Which means I'm not going to stop trying to whip you into shape." She picked up a bottle of styling mousse. "If you'll just let me fluff your hair out a little and put some spray on, it'll help."

Jane took a swift step back and held up her hands. "I hate that stuff. It makes me sneeze."

Ellen stepped forward. "Sometimes you have to suffer in the name of beauty."

Again Jane backed away, her boots scraping softly on the checkered tile floor. "I wouldn't wind up anywhere near a beauty if you sprayed the whole can on me."

Her taller and curvier sister raised a well-arched brow. "As I've told you I don't know how many times, you could look better—a *lot* better—if you'd take some pointers from me."

"I'm happy as I am," Jane said firmly. Maybe there were times she couldn't help but wish she bore at least a passing resemblance to some of the models featured on the covers of glossy magazines like those strewn about the salon's waiting area. But seeing a model's face in her own mirror was a fantasy, she realized. The reality of the situation—her reality— was that nature had dealt her a far different hand.

Ellen set the can down. "Defeated again," she grumbled.

"You'll survive," Jane told her in a bolstering tone.

"Uh-huh." Ellen met her sister's gaze. "But how will you fare tangling with a good-looking consultant?"

It was Jane's turn to frown. "I didn't say he was good-looking."

"You didn't have to," Ellen said with a knowing glint in her deep green eyes, "because I remember what you told me before you even got a glimpse of him—that he's related to one of Harmony's founding families. His last name might be Lassiter, but he's also part Hayward, and all the Haywards are attractive.''

"Maybe he's the exception."

"Is he?"

"No," Jane had to concede. "He's attractive enough...if you like the dressed-for-success type."

"The type you've never had much experience dealing with before," Ellen pointed out.

"Which doesn't mean I can't handle it—and him."

"Mmm-hmm," Ellen murmured, her expression becoming thoughtful. "I do believe Miss Hester was right. It'll be *real* interesting to see how the two of you handle each other."

Privately, Jane thought so, too, and despite her outward show of bravado, inwardly she wasn't quite so certain of being able to hold her own. It was a good thing—a double-darn good thing, she told herself—that she had one big advantage. However much time she and Adam Lassiter spent together this summer, they would spend it on her turf. Not his. Still, for as much comfort as that brought, her worries remained centered on one question.

Would Glory Ridge survive?

Chapter Two

Adam flicked off the air conditioner and rolled down the windows of the blue hatchback sedan he'd rented. "Smell that pine-scented air," he said in a hearty tone. It sounded a little forced, but at least he was making an effort to hold a conversation, which was more than his son had done since they'd left busy Phoenix behind them.

"Uh-huh," Sam said, and scrunched lower in his seat.

Even then Adam noted that his son's head, topped by short, light-brown hair, came up higher than it had a year earlier. That was the first thing he'd recognized on picking Sam up at the airport less than two weeks ago—how he'd grown. Not long afterward, the second truth to hit was that their mostly long-distance relationship was taking its toll. He and Sam were losing the connection that had been uniquely theirs from the day Adam had first held a red-faced baby in his arms.

That realization had shaken him badly. He could still recall the chill it had sent sliding down his spine.

"I know you're not thrilled about postponing Disneyland to come up here," Adam said, deciding to tackle the issue before they got to their destination. "The thing is, we've been there more than once, and spending some time in the mountains will be a first for you." *Plus spending some quiet time together instead of the usual round of summer activities I turned to in an effort to entertain you might do us both some good,* he thought.

"Uh-huh," Sam muttered again, patently unenthused by the prospect of a get-acquainted session with the great outdoors.

Okay, so maybe his son wasn't the only one who was failing to work up much enthusiasm in that regard, Adam conceded. They were both roughing it anyway. He might be wrong about this being his best chance to reestablish a closer bond between them, but it was worth a shot. Right now, he had to believe that.

"What did your mother have to say when you phoned her this morning?" Adam asked in another bid to keep the conversation going. He had no intention of mentioning that he'd spent a good part of the past several nights staring up at the ceiling and wondering if his ex-wife's recent remarriage could somehow be a factor in the wall his son had built around himself.

Sam tapped the heels of his running shoes together. "She said I should be careful playing in the woods." He paused. "She didn't sound so good."

Adam frowned and glanced toward the passenger's seat. "What do you mean?"

Shrugging, Sam said, "Like maybe she was a little sick or something."

"Well, she could have caught a bug, I suppose." Adam slowed to negotiate a sharp turn in a road winding steadily upward. "You know you can call her on my cell phone whenever you want to while we're away, but I don't think there's anything to worry about. Your mother's always taken good care of herself and eaten healthy foods, even when she's dieting."

"I think she eats more than she used to," Sam offered after a beat. "I heard her say something about buying bigger clothes."

Ariel? Letting her model-slim figure go? Adam had a hard time imagining that. Still, he said nothing. What he'd really like to discuss was Sam's relationship with his new stepfather, but something told him he wouldn't win any real confidences, not yet, and the last thing he wanted was pat answers.

"Speaking of clothes," he said, "how do those jeans feel?"

"Okay, I guess." Sam looked down at one of three pairs of blue jeans bought during a whirlwind trip through the mall the day before. "They're sort of stiff."

"They won't be once they're washed," Adam assured him. The same applied to his own dark Levi's and black denim shirt, he imagined, both of which bore little resemblance to the knit shirts and cotton slacks he favored as casual clothing. His new boots would need some breaking in, too. But a few days of trekking through the pines would take care of that, even though he had always preferred jogging on the track at his health club to hiking anywhere—much less through a forest. Nevertheless, he would do it— with his son at his side.

"Once we get our bearings, we'll be glad we added to our wardrobe. We'll hike our way through the woods and do a fine job of it," Adam contended with a determined set of his jaw.

"Uh-huh," Sam muttered one more time with clear misgivings as they reached the faded wooden sign pointing the way to Glory Ridge Resort and Campground.

In a matter of minutes Adam brought the sedan to a stop in the gravel lot next to the resort's office. Only feet away stood the dusty red pickup belonging to the resort's owner, which had been parked there on his earlier visit. "We're here," he said.

Sam sat up straight and glanced out through the windshield. In the next breath, his jaw dropped like a stone. "Dad, there's a skunk on the porch!"

Dad. For a silent moment Adam closed his eyes in sheer gratefulness at hearing that word from his son's lips—a word he'd been waiting for ever since Sam had stepped off the airplane looking more wary than happy to see his father. Right this minute, he could only be glad—damn glad—that he'd made the decision to come to a place so foreign to both of them.

"It's okay," he said. "The skunk is basically harmless, I'm told."

Moving with caution despite that assurance, Sam stuck his head out the car window. "I don't smell nothing."

"You don't smell *anything,*" Adam said, automatically correcting his son, "because the skunk doesn't have the usual equipment."

"You mean he's lost his stinker?"

"Actually, it's a she," Adam explained, "and yes, she's lost her, uh, stinker."

"Boy, the guys in school will never believe this."
Sam looked back at Adam. "Can I take a picture?"

"Sure."

The one thing Sam seemed genuinely enthusiastic
about these days was the camera his father had sent
him for Christmas. *At least you did well there, Lassiter,* Adam told himself. He got out of the car, then
walked around to open Sam's door. The little boy
grabbed his camera from the back seat and hopped
to the ground.

The skunk calmly waddled down the steps and approached the new arrivals. "Her name is Sweet
Pea," Adam said dryly.

Sam carefully aimed his camera and took a picture, after which Sweet Pea gave both males a brief
sniff and strolled off toward the trees. "You were
right," the eight-year-old whispered, watching the
animal's departure, "this place is like nowhere I've
ever been."

Adam didn't add that Sam was about to meet a
woman who probably bore little resemblance to anyone he'd ever met, either. He set a hand gently on
his son's shoulder and urged him toward the cabin.
"Let's see if the owner is in her office."

Sam glanced around him as they climbed the
porch steps. "Does she like living all the way out
here?"

"Yes, she does," Adam replied, sure of his words.

"Why?"

"Because she's different from the kind of people
who prefer living in towns and cities."

Sam sighed mournfully. "Maybe she thinks it's
okay, but I bet there's nowhere close around to even
get the kinda hamburgers and fries I like."

Adam recognized this reference to his son's favorite fast-food restaurant, where they'd stopped for lunch before heading for the wilds of the mountains. "No, I'm afraid not," he said.

Sam's dark mood, lightened by the unexpected sight of Sweet Pea, seemed to return as he sighed again.

JANE STOOD IN THE rear of the cabin, surveying what she considered a job well done. She'd just completed rearranging the furniture to transform the room into an office for two. One of twin swivel chairs that continued to creak despite her liberal use of oil stood behind the small desk that had been cleared of everything but an antique brass banker's lamp. The other chair sat behind an old card table, set up to face the desk and hold the combination answering machine and phone. Her consultant now had a desk at his disposal and could hook up to the phone line whenever he needed to, she thought with satisfaction, turning to welcome her guests with a polite smile when the cabin door opened. Her smile swiftly widened as she took in Adam Lassiter dressed in an obviously brand-new outfit, looking a long way from comfortable in crisp black denim.

Out of his element, she reflected with amusement. Not that he wasn't still attractive. He was. But he no longer appeared so self-assured, and that somehow pleased her, honesty forced her to admit.

"I was expecting you about now," she said. For a moment her gaze met his across the room. Then she dropped it to the boy standing at his father's side. Stepping forward, she held out a hand. "I'm Jane

Pitt. We don't waste much time using last names around here, so feel free to call me Jane.''

"I'm Sam," the child replied after a beat, and placed his hand in hers for a brief handshake. Although his hair was shades lighter than Adam's, his gray eyes were a duplicate of the man who had fathered him. "I already met your skunk. I heard she lost her stinker.''

Jane nodded. "That's right. Only thing to smell around here is the pines." And a whiff of men's cologne, she added to herself. The fancy suit might be gone, but he still wore an expensive sandalwood scent. Taking a short step back, she studied the two males staring at her. "I've got your cabin all ready for you.''

"I never stayed in a cabin before," Sam confided.

And he didn't seem too happy about staying in one now, Jane noted. She didn't miss the fact that his jeans were as brand-new as his father's. They'd probably gone on a hasty shopping trip to get ready for their visit to Glory Ridge.

Why, she had to ask herself one more time, had Adam decided to bring his son here? Again no ready answer came to mind. Yet, whatever his reasons, they'd arrived as promised—which suited her purposes, Jane reminded herself. So there was no sense wasting time puzzling about it.

"Staying in a cabin could be fun," she told Sam. "You can pretend you're back in an earlier time.''

Sam's mouth drooped at the corners. "They didn't have any rockets or spaceships back then." And rockets and spaceships were what fired this boy's imagination. Both his expression and the colorful images on his *Star Wars* T-shirt testified to that.

"Well, let's get unpacked," Adam said, his deep voice underscored with resignation, as though he believed Jane was fighting a losing battle in trying to put an upbeat slant on the situation.

Abandoning her effort, she followed them out the door. She smiled wryly when her gaze landed on the car parked in the lot. "No sleek black sports model today, hmm?" she murmured to Adam as Sam headed down the porch steps.

"I thought it would be smarter to rent something else. Besides, there wasn't room for our luggage and the rest of the stuff I had to bring."

She recalled yesterday's phone conversation, during which she'd reminded him that he'd have to provide for his personal needs while he was at the resort. Glory Ridge had plenty of sporting equipment for guests to use, but... "I hope you remembered that meals aren't a part of the deal."

He looked down at her. "I brought some food to cook—don't worry."

She raised an eyebrow skeptically. "*Can* you cook?" She'd willingly bet that this man had grown up with a housekeeper to fix the family meals.

"I get by," he told her. And that was all he said before he started for his car.

Jane shrugged. Whether he could cook was hardly her concern. "I'd be glad to give you a hand getting settled in," she offered, as she would to any guest.

Adam kept on moving. "Okay," he said, tossing the word over his shoulder. At the moment, he had to admit he was far from sure how he felt about Glory Ridge's owner. He knew she was amused by the fact that surroundings so familiar to her were strange to him—just as she had been on the day they'd met. But he also knew that she'd attempted to make his son welcome, so he supposed he'd try not to let her amusement annoy him.

Besides, he thought with satisfaction, once they got down to business, his considerable experience in dealing with a world mostly foreign to her would display his talents. Even if he couldn't pull off a miracle with Glory Ridge, he'd at least show her a thing or two.

Adam opened the hatchback trunk and pulled out two suitcases, plus twin canvas backpacks, the store tags still on. He handed the backpacks to Sam, then pushed aside two paper shopping bags filled with food and hefted a large cooler into his arms. "If you'll take the grocery bags," he told Jane, "I'll come back for the suitcases."

"I can take the suitcases," she told him.

"They're heavy," he said. "Leave them for me to handle."

She planted her hands on slender hips once again covered by battered blue denim and met his gaze. "I can handle them, trust me. I'm stronger—a *lot* stronger—than I look."

"Well, nature usually favoring the male of the species," he said with undeniable relish, "I'm even stronger than you are, so leave the suitcases for me." With that, he stared her down until she retrieved the grocery bags and started up the gravel path to the cabins, Sam following a step behind.

Feeling better at having won that last round, Adam brought up the rear. Even his new boots felt better, he acknowledged with the beginnings of a smile. But that faint smile disappeared as he approached the cabin and got another look at the place where he and his son would be sleeping, bathing and eating.

Although he hadn't gone into details earlier, he did know how to cook. In fact, since his divorce and return to single status, he'd become a man who could hold his own in the kitchen. Trouble was, none of his specialties—acclaimed by his occasional dinner guests—seemed to tempt the taste buds of a growing boy, so he and Sam usually went out to eat or brought something in.

Not that he was feeling guilty about his failure to produce homemade meals to meet his son's tastes. Sam probably didn't get much homemade fare back in Boston, either. Ariel had certainly never been keen on doing much cooking.

Adam blew out a breath. No, he wouldn't feel guilty. He just wished they stood a chance of getting a pizza delivered out here every now and then—and knew they didn't.

"Why is that old sign nailed over the door?" Sam asked.

"Because Squirrel Hollow is the name of this cabin," Jane explained. "It's been called that from the day it was first built."

Sam conducted a short study and shook his head sadly. "That must've been a long time ago."

"Yes," she acknowledged mildly. "Want to get the screen door? Your father and I sort of have our hands full."

Silent now, Sam slowly climbed the steps, as though headed toward a harsh fate. He held the screen door ajar, then stood back as Adam and Jane entered.

"I left the other door and the windows open to air the place out," she said.

Adam could hardly argue the wisdom of that plan, or that the breeze drifting through the place felt good, especially after leaving the hot desert regions to the south. "You can put the backpacks on one of the chairs by the fireplace," he said to Sam. Then he strode to the kitchen area adjoining the living room and set the cooler on the tiled counter.

"I can start unloading the groceries if you want to show Sam the rest of the place," Jane suggested.

"All right." Adam brushed his palms on his Levi's. "Let's check it out," he told his son, and walked beside the boy toward the back of the cabin.

"This is where I'll be sleeping," he said as they poked their heads into the bigger of the two bedrooms. There a sturdy pine bed and small nightstand shared space with a mirror-topped dresser, also made of rough-hewn pine, that stood midway between a single bare window and a narrow closet.

"And this will be your room," he added moments later as they inspected the second bedroom, slightly smaller than the first. It, too, had a pine dresser, and a bunk bed with a short ladder propped against it to reach the upper bunk.

"You get to decide whether to sleep on the top or bottom." Once again Adam tried for an enthusiastic tone, but his effort fell flat, met by a strained silence.

Finally, Sam walked in, dragging his feet every step of the way, and tossed his camera on the plaid wool blanket covering the lower bunk. "I'll take this one, I guess."

"Good." Adam felt a stab of sympathy, but steeled himself against giving in to it. He wasn't any fonder of his sleeping accommodations, but he and Sam would get through this, he assured himself, and with any luck at all become closer in the process.

God, he had to hope that would happen.

"I know it's not what you're used to," he went on with determination, "but this cabin could be considered a part of the history of this area. You might want to take some pictures of the place later."

The swift roll of Sam's eyes said, *You've got to be kidding!* as clearly as if he'd spoken the words.

Adam let the subject drop with a slight shrug and turned from the doorway. "The bathroom's down this way."

It took them less than a minute to view the old sink, toilet and tub. They returned to the kitchen and found Jane still emptying a tall grocery bag. "I put the cereal, bread and canned stuff in the cabinet by the stove," she said. "Candy bars are in the top drawer next to the refrigerator."

"I could use a candy bar," Sam mumbled with a sidelong glance up at his father.

"You can have one," Adam said. At least, he reflected with more than a little irony, his son hadn't lost his appetite.

Sam made his choice and took a seat at the square, Formica-topped table. He stared out a side window at a high wall of deep green forest and seemed to get lost in his thoughts.

Jane continued with her project. After pulling out a long, narrow box, she squinted at the label. "This looks like spaghetti, but I've never seen this brand before."

"It's imported from Italy," Adam explained.

"Oh." Her lips quirked. "Should have known."

There was no reason for that comment to put his teeth on edge, Adam told himself as he opened the cooler and hauled out a gallon of milk and a six-pack of the cola Sam favored. He set a short supply of the bottled spring water he liked on the counter, then reached in and retrieved one of the bottles of wine he'd removed from a chrome rack in his large, modern kitchen that morning.

Jane's gaze landed on the wine as she folded the now-empty grocery bag. "I guess that's imported, too, huh?"

"Yes." The word came out more clipped than he'd intended. He gave himself a second to regroup, then asked, oh-so-casually, "Do you like wine?"

She met his eyes. "When I'm in the mood for alcohol, I mostly drink beer—and not the imported kind."

Of course she would. And so would many of the people who had occupied this cabin before him, Adam imagined. Well, he was different. And he wasn't going to apologize for it.

"To each his own," he said.

"Mmm-hmm." She turned, reached into the remaining grocery bag and began to stack salad fixings on the counter. "I think you forgot the lettuce," she remarked after a moment.

"There's lettuce." Adam set down another bottle of wine and pointed to a leafy green bundle. "That's romaine."

"Oh, a fancy lettuce."

Jane didn't roll her eyes as his son had earlier, but Adam had little doubt she wanted to. That threatened to put his teeth on edge for a second time. "I can handle the rest of the groceries," he told her.

"Okay." She stepped away from the counter and looked at Sam. "Bye for now," she said with a friendly smile that became merely polite as she returned her gaze to Adam. "You can get settled in the office whenever it suits you." She pulled two keys from a jeans pocket and handed them over. "One's for this cabin. The other's for the office if I'm not around."

He dropped them into one of the front pockets of his new shirt. "I'll show Sam the rest of the resort before I fix dinner. I may get a chance to set up at the office later tonight."

Jane nodded. "If you need anything that I haven't thought of, my cabin's not far away. Just start walking toward the lake and take a left when you come to a small fork in the path. The place is hard to see through the trees, but it's easy enough to find when you know it's there."

"Does yours have a name, too?" Sam asked after a last swallow of his candy bar.

"Sure does. It's Pitt's Pride."

Appropriate, Adam thought, more than suspecting that Jane Pitt had her share of pride and then some, as her great-aunt had probably had before her. "I'll find it if I have to," he said.

"Flashlight's in the bottom cabinet next to the sink," she told him. "Be sure to use it if you're roaming around after dark. Won't do anybody any good if you wind up getting lost in the woods."

Adam crossed his arms over his chest and stared down at her, his gaze narrowing. "I don't plan on getting lost," he replied firmly. He, too, had his share of pride. More than enough to reject even the remote possibility of losing his way.

Shrugging, she gave the items stacked on the counter a last look and headed for the porch.

"Way out of his element," he heard her mutter before the screen door shut behind her with a thud.

JANE DIDN'T REALLY EXPECT to see a light on in the office when she went for a walk after dinner. She'd already watched the sunset from her kitchen window—something that had become a habit well before she'd switched cabins and moved into Pitt's Pride after Aunt Maude was gone. To her, taking in that eye-pleasing sight and following it up with a quiet stroll just as the stars were making their appearance was the best way to end the day.

But despite how she favored spending her time before retiring for the night, she'd figured the resort's new arrivals would take another tack and turn in early on their first evening at Glory Ridge. Apparently, she was wrong, because someone was in the office, and it could only be Adam Lassiter.

She could just continue on her walk. Truth was, he'd probably prefer it. She'd noticed that he'd been far from thrilled with her comments on his grocery choices, not to mention her suggestion that he might get lost in the woods. Then again, she could always act as if she'd noted nothing and give in to the growing urge to see what he was up to. In the end, curiosity won out and had her investigating.

She found him seated behind the desk, his attention fixed on his laptop computer. The white glow from its small screen, together with the brass banker's lamp at his elbow, provided more than enough light to make out his chiseled profile.

"Hi," she said with deliberate casualness as she

leaned in the doorway. "I thought maybe you'd leave the computer stuff until tomorrow."

He glanced her way. "It seemed wiser to get a start on my research, since I had some time to myself. With no television up here, Sam decided to head off to his room and read for a while."

"What does he like to read?" she asked. Reading had always been a pleasure of hers.

His mouth slanted wryly. "Science fiction, what else."

"Hmm. Well, it fits right in with rockets and spaceships," Jane allowed. With that, she took several steps forward, pulled out the remaining chair and sat facing her consultant behind the card table backed up to the front of the desk. "It's none of my business, I'll admit, but he looks a long way from pleased to be spending part of his summer here."

He studied her for a moment. "I don't know how much experience you have with children—"

"Not a whole lot," she readily conceded, breaking in. "My sister has a son around Sam's age. And kids have visited Glory Ridge off and on. Other than that, I haven't spent much time with the younger set, but—"

It was his turn to interrupt. "I hope you'll recognize that having been Sam's father for eight years, I do have considerable experience, at least where he's concerned."

And how my son feels is my concern, not yours. He didn't voice those words, but she heard them anyway. And hadn't she already admitted Sam was none of her business?

"Point taken," Jane said. She changed subjects. "What kind of research do you plan on doing?"

His broad shoulders, which had stiffened for a minute, relaxed. "First thing on the agenda is to check out the resort's competition—exactly who's located where, what they charge and what they have to offer. Then I'll try to dig a little deeper and find out who's making a consistent profit, who's not and why. Once that's done, I'll have a better idea what this place is up against."

She ran her tongue around her teeth. "Sounds like a smart way to kick things off." Honesty forced her to concede.

"When it comes to business, smart is my middle name." It was no rash boast, just a soft and simple statement that rang with conviction. "I've helped both large and small companies throughout the western United States enhance their strengths and eliminate their weaknesses. Sometimes, it takes an outsider to get an objective analysis. And my suggestions have usually produced sizable profits."

She leaned back in her swivel chair, which offered a squeak of protest. "Well, I guess they don't pay you the big bucks for nothing."

He grinned a wide grin—the first she'd seen crossing his face and one that instantly brought to mind Hester Goodbody's words about her former pupil: *He was a charmer.*

Yes, Jane could see it now. And, she told herself, she could also pay that charm no mind. If she wasn't quite as successful at that as she hoped to be, the last thing she wanted to do was let him know it. She sat silently while the old alarm clock standing on one of the file cabinets ticked off several seconds. "Could be you just might wind up earning your free stay here,'' she went on at last in the most offhand manner she could summon.

Still grinning, he replied, "At the rate I normally charge for my services, it would take me less than a day to do that.''

"Humph." Again she fought a war with her curiosity before it won out. "How much do you usually charge?''

The figure he named had her eyes round. "For a *day?*''

"Mmm-hmm. Plus expenses, of course.''

No wonder he could afford to drive a fancy sports car and wear suits that had never come off a rack. His parents might be well-to-do, but he seemed to be making his own way—and doing a bang-up job of it. Jane had to respect that, even if she didn't plan on saying as much. "What happens after your research on the resort's competition is done?''

His grin faded and his expression became all business. "Then we put our heads together and come up with a marketing strategy to take advantage of what I've learned.''

Once again she couldn't fault the wisdom of his plan. He obviously knew what he was doing. She was the one who'd have to meet the challenge of keeping up with him. For all that she'd gotten good grades, she had never considered going on to college after high school. None of the Pitts had a college education.

Adam Lassiter, on the other hand, had probably not only aced his classes but wound up with a degree. Maybe more than one. And even beyond being educated, he could well be judged as having earned the title "expert.''

But only when it came to business, she reminded herself. In other areas, she could lay claim to being an expert. And maybe a demonstration was in order.

"I take it you and Sam also came here to spend some time outdoors," she said. "Since you've made a start on your research this evening, how about a little fishing tomorrow?"

He hesitated for a beat. "Tomorrow?"

"Sure." Thunder rumbled in the distance as she propped an elbow on the table and set her chin in the palm of her hand.

"Maybe it'll be raining," he replied after another hesitation—and with what just might be a hint of hope that would happen. "I remember how often storms whipping down from the mountains used to blow through Harmony in the summer."

She shook her head. "The rains are late this year. It's been thundering a ways off for the past several evenings, but we haven't had a drop lately—and the forecast on the radio this morning was for more sunny skies tomorrow. I can take you and Sam out on the lake and give you a few pointers in the fishing department. That's what I did for years when my great-aunt was still in charge around here—act as a guide on and off when visitors requested one."

He released what sounded like a resigned breath, then set his jaw, as though having resolved to tackle something he was hardly eager to do.

"All right," he said.

"Good." She shoved back her chair and got to her feet. "I keep our extra fishing equipment in the storage room," she explained with a nod at a doorway off one side of the office. "I'll pull out what you two need first thing tomorrow and meet you here at five o'clock.''

His eyes widened for a second, then narrowed in a flash. "Five in the *morning?*"

She held back a smile. "That's when the fish start biting."

He let out another breath, pressed a few keys that made the computer screen fade to black and closed the laptop with a snap. "I suppose I'll turn in," he said, rising.

"A smart man probably would," she told him, doing her best to maintain a bland expression.

He picked up the flashlight lying on the desk, switched it on and turned off the lamp. Seconds later he was locking the outside door behind them. As he aimed the flashlight down the gravel path, they walked toward his cabin. At the porch, a faint glow spilled through the front windows, over the rocking chair set beside the door. Several yards away, an owl hooted in the trees, the only sound in the quiet surroundings.

"Well, I guess this is where we part company," she said.

He flicked off the flashlight. "Want to take this with you?"

She shook her head. "I can do without, especially with the stars out. Even when they're not, I don't have much trouble. I know my way around this place."

He didn't argue the point. "Then I'll see you tomorrow."

"At five," she cheerfully reminded him.

Even in the dim light, she didn't miss his fleeting grimace before he held out his right hand in an apparent effort to put things back on a businesslike basis. "Good night."

"Good night," she said, and placed her hand in his for the first time. As she'd expected, his palm was warm and dry and not at all rough to the touch. What she didn't expect—despite the ease with which he'd handled the large cooler earlier that day—was the solid strength underscoring his light grasp. Or how the feel of his bare skin against hers would affect her.

Because it did.

Jane dragged in a steadying stream of cool air and pulled her hand away. *Get moving,* she flat-out ordered herself. *And while you're at it, get your head screwed on straight.*

Obeying at least that first command, she turned and continued down the path that would fork off to her cabin. With firm determination to betray nothing out of the ordinary, she didn't so much as toss a backward glance over her shoulder. Still, there was no denying the blunt truth that she had felt some sort of…attraction, she guessed would describe it. One that all boiled down to male and female. She'd seen too much of nature's ways to fail to recognize it.

Good grief, for that brief yet humming moment when their palms had touched, she'd been in danger of being bowled over in the most barnyard-basic way by Adam Lassiter—probably the fanciest man she'd ever met. As a plain woman, she knew down to the familiar ground under her feet how foolish that was.

She'd only made a fool of herself once before over a good-looking male, and that was so far back it didn't really count. Not that she didn't recall the times she'd let Bobby Breen sweet-talk her into the back seat of his old Chevy convertible. Or how he had moved on when a prettier girl took an interest. Still, she'd survived that stinging rejection and come out the wiser.

All she had to do was keep that in mind from now on when dealing with a slick consultant. He probably wouldn't be sporting any charming grins come morning, Jane assured herself. More likely, he'd be half-asleep.

She, however, was used to getting up early. And she could be chipper, too, at that time of day. Which she would be tomorrow, she vowed. She wasn't letting anyone in on the fact that if she and Adam Lassiter had shaken hands during his first visit to Glory Ridge, she might never have encouraged him to spend part of his summer here, much as she needed some savvy business advice.

No, she wasn't letting anyone know that.

Especially him.

Chapter Three

"Good morning, early risers," a resonant voice greeted over the airwaves. "We're still a bit shy of sunrise, folks, but it looks as though yesterday's weather forecast was right on target. All signs are that it's going to be another beautiful day in Harmony."

Adam met that news, delivered by the far-from-new clock radio standing on the bedroom dresser, with a groan. WHAR, one of two stations vying for listeners from among Harmony's residents, had jarred him out of a sound sleep—and he wasn't happy about it.

"Why would any fish with half a brain want to put itself in danger of being caught this early?" he grumbled. It didn't help that he'd spent too long getting to sleep the night before, a circumstance he was inclined to lay at Jane Pitt's door, for all that it didn't make a lot of sense.

Whether it made sense or not, he had to admit that something had happened just before she'd headed off to her cabin. Something that had made him aware that she was a woman—and not a prickly one, either.

Adam frowned, thinking back to how he'd

watched as she'd disappeared into the darkness, and how, for a few fleeting moments that continued to mystify him, he'd been reluctant to see her go. Logic said that he should have been glad to do without any more of her cheery reminders of the fishing expedition in his immediate future. He should, in fact, have released a grateful breath on her departure. But he hadn't. Not last night.

His lack of gratitude must be a fluke.

Assuring himself that could only be the case, Adam propped his eyes open and discovered that it was still pitch-black in the bedroom and outside, as well. He stared up at the ceiling, recalling the dream that had captured his mind once sleep had finally claimed him. The same dream he'd had several times in the past, although he hadn't had it for a while. In it, he strode down a long corridor filled with closed doors on both sides. One by one, he opened them, searching for something—exactly what, he'd never been able to grasp. He only knew that he'd failed to find that elusive *something,* again and again. The dream always left him with an empty, hollow feeling, and he'd been glad to be free of it.

But now that dream had come back. And he had no idea why.

Resolutely setting thoughts of it aside, he fumbled for the switch on a small bedside lamp and got out of bed.

"To get your day off to a rousing start, here's an oldie but goodie from the Rolling Stones," the announcer informed his listeners. The first notes of "Jumpin' Jack Flash" boomed out, then died to silence as Adam shut off the radio. He took off the gray sweats he was using for pajamas, then pulled on clean underwear and fresh socks, plus the same pair of Levi's and black denim shirt he'd worn the day before. Once he'd shoved his feet into his new boots, his next stop was the bathroom. He washed his face but didn't bother to shave, then rapped on the door to his son's room and poked his head inside.

"Time to get up," he said, not even attempting a hearty tone. He already knew, thanks to a brief and hardly happy conversation the evening before on his return to the cabin, that Sam was no more eager than he was to crawl out of bed far earlier than either of them was used to getting up. But they were doing it anyway. Adam had been firm on that score. Their spending time together without the frenzied activities of prior summers had been his goal, and if joining forces to haul in a fish could accomplish that, then so be it.

"It's still dark," Sam mumbled after turning over and blinking at the hall light Adam had switched on.

"It probably won't be for much longer," Adam replied, although he had no idea what time the sun actually rose. Still, given that it was summer, the sky was bound to show some light soon. Cripes, he had to hope so.

"I'll have breakfast on the table by the time you wash up and get dressed," he went on, and paid no attention to more mumbling that followed as he headed for the kitchen. A glance at his watch told him that by the time he figured out how to make coffee in the old-fashioned percolator sitting on a stove burner he wouldn't have much chance to drink it if he planned to meet Jane at the office at five. Which he did. He had no intention of allowing her to be smug about his being late.

Not when she'll probably be early, he told himself. Even on short acquaintance, he imagined that was a pretty sure bet.

It was still dark after he and Sam ate their twin bowls of cold cereal, mainly in a groggy silence, and left the cabin. Adam again used the flashlight to help him find his way, and they arrived at the office a few minutes before five. As he'd expected, Jane Pitt was already there. What he didn't expect, however, was the smell of freshly brewed coffee that had his mouth watering from the moment his nose caught a whiff.

Jane sat behind the desk with a thick stoneware mug in hand, wearing a blue and white checked shirt and a frayed navy baseball cap that might have been older than she was. "I see you're right on time." She was chipper.

Way too chipper, as far as Adam was concerned. "Actually, we're a little early," it pleased him to reply, although he couldn't match her tone. He doubted many people could at a godforsaken hour of the morning when even the birds weren't up yet. Standing next to him, small hands shoved into the pockets of his new jeans, Sam only yawned a wide yawn that said he for one remained far from awake, never mind alert.

Jane gave the boy a small, knowing smile, then lifted her mug. "Want another dose of caffeine before we get started?" she asked Adam.

"Sure," he said. He didn't mention it would be his first of the day—or that a part of him less determined to let pride rule was urging him to get down on his knees in sheer thankfulness. Instead, he wasted no time in heading for the coffeemaker. He picked up another of the heavy mugs stacked beside it and poured himself a hefty helping of dark, fragrant brew. A few sips had his eyes no longer in danger of drooping.

"This is good," he told Jane.

She met his gaze over the rim of her mug. "I can make coffee."

"Mmm-hmm." He had to admit that it tasted like some of the best he'd ever had.

"I pulled out some fishing poles and other equipment for you and Sam," she added with a nod toward one side of the room.

He looked in the direction she'd indicated and saw two metal poles, one half the size of the other, leaning against the wall. A dented, dull green tackle box and a small white net he assumed was used to scoop up a fish once it was hooked rested on the floor nearby. Memories of the few times he'd headed for the large lagoon at Harmony Park as a young boy with a simple bamboo pole and the hope of catching something came back to him. He'd never had much success and had soon lost interest. If anyone had predicted only weeks earlier that he'd be making another attempt this summer, he'd have questioned their sanity.

He returned his gaze to Jane. "Are you fishing, too?"

She shook her head and rose to her feet. "I'll be a guide today. We'd better get started. The sun should be on its way up any minute."

After polishing off his coffee, Adam crossed the room, picked up the poles and handed the shorter one to Sam, who inspected it with clear misgivings.

"What do we put on the hook?" he asked Jane.

"We'll start out with worms and see how it goes."

Sam frowned. "Do we hafta dig 'em up?"

"Not today." Jane shut off the coffeemaker. "I've got some in the refrigerator."

Sam's eyes flew to meet Adam's. "Is she kidding?" he asked in a whisper as Jane started for the outer room.

"Trust me, she's not," Adam murmured in return. He bent to retrieve the net and passed it to Sam. "You take this. I'll take the tackle box. And I suppose she'll take the worms," he added with a large dose of irony.

A FIRST FEW faint rays of light visible to the east guided their way down the path toward the lake. Jane had put several cans of soda and the coffee can holding the worms into an older, far smaller cooler than the one the Lassiters had brought with them. Swinging it by its short handle, she took the lead and held her head high.

The day was off to as good a start as could be expected, she decided. Nothing in her expression or her voice had betrayed anything of what she'd felt during that handshake the evening before. Thinking back over the past several minutes, she was sure of it. And that was the most important thing. While her consultant might look even more appealing in a dangerously male sort of fashion with a night's growth of dark beard, he had no idea she thought so—and she planned to keep it that way.

Once they reached Quail Lake, Jane set the cooler down on the grassy shore a few feet from the water. "We need to try some casting before we take out a boat," she said.

"Casting?" Sam repeated with a puzzled look.

That she'd have to start from scratch came as little surprise. "That's what it's called when you throw your fishing line into the water and reel it in—hopefully with a good-sized trout on the other end." Jane reached up and tugged down the bill of her ball cap. "I won't deny that a bit of luck doesn't hurt when it comes to catching anything, but it helps—a lot—to know what you're doing."

Which they didn't. That became as clear as glass when father and son attempted a trial cast after a few initial instructions. Sam's hook plopped into the water scarce inches from the bank. Adam's never made it that far. Instead, his fishing line wound up wrapped around the branch of a tall tree a few feet behind him.

Jane ignored what might have been a muttered oath too low to be distinct. "Good backward action," she said dryly to the man at her side. "But you're not supposed to let the line go until you snap your wrist to start your forward motion."

He frowned up at the tree. "So you told me."

She swallowed the urge to chuckle. "Just a reminder."

"Point taken," he replied after a beat. "Now, how the hell—" He glanced at his son. "How the heck do I get it out of there?"

She took the long pole from him and gave it a practiced jerk that freed the line, then handed it back to him. A rueful grimace on his part wouldn't have surprised her. Truth be told, she would have enjoyed seeing one cross his face.

Instead, he was staring over her shoulder with an expression far more engrossed than rueful. Following his gaze, she discovered what had captured his attention. The newly dawning sun was just skirting the top of the low mountain that rose to a gentle peak on one side of the lake.

For the next few minutes, she divided her attention between that familiar sight and her companions. She quickly saw that Adam wasn't the only one who found the sunrise fascinating. For the first time that morning, Sam's eyes were fully open as he stood stock-still and studied the tips of the trees being lit with a hazy glow.

In that moment, Jane felt surprisingly close to her guests—mostly, she supposed, because viewing that sunrise with wonder was a feeling she could understand, and share. Then the spell was broken as a fish jumped in the water and landed with a soft splash.

"Was that a trout?" Sam asked, eyes still wide.

"Probably," Jane replied. "There are some bass in the lake, but more trout, for sure. And right now most of them are looking for breakfast. Once we get out on the lake, we'll see if we can tempt a keeper to sample one of our worms."

"A keeper?" Again Sam's expression was puzzled.

"A fish that's big enough to keep. If they're returned to the water quickly enough, they usually swim off, no worse for the experience."

"They probably just get smarter about taking a hook the next time around," Adam ventured with a shrewd glint in his gaze.

"I'd say you're right," Jane allowed. She looked at Sam. "There's one fat trout living in Quail Lake— Clever Clyde, we call him—who's been outsmarting fishermen for quite a while. That's what makes catching bigger fish a challenge."

Soon both her guests were casting with better results—especially Adam. Watching how with each attempt his long arm and strong wrist sent the line
snapping forward to fly on a straighter and farther
path before it met the lake, she couldn't deny he was
a fast learner.

"I think I've got the hang of it," he said with
undeniable satisfaction.

Jane didn't disagree, but she knew there was more
to landing a fish than casting a line. A lot more.
"Since you seem to be confident enough—" *not to
mention just a bit smug,* she thought, "—I'll concentrate on helping Sam once we take the boat out."

He met her gaze. His swiftly narrowed, as if he'd
caught the trace of a dare to go it alone in her matter-
of-fact statement. "That's fine with me."

Realizing her words had indeed been a dare, one
she hadn't been able to resist, she said, "Great." She
bent to pick up the cooler resting on the bank. "First
lesson when we get out on the lake is how to bait a
hook," she told Sam.

"Okay," he agreed, sounding at least a bit more
enthusiastic. After retrieving the net he'd been carrying, he fell into step beside her as they walked
down the old wooden dock. "Why do fish want to
eat so early?" he asked with the barest hint of a
grumble.

"Beats me," she replied. "They just do."

"Are we gonna take a boat with a motor?"

She mulled that over for a moment, weighing the
merits of using one of the ancient outboard motors
against putting a pair of oars to good use. "The motors are pretty noisy and we're not going all the way
across the lake, so I guess I'll row us out."

"I can row," a low voice said from behind her.

Jane aimed a glance back at Adam. "It takes some practice. Otherwise, you can wind up going around in circles."

"I was on a rowing team in college," he said, looking pleased to relay that information. "I can row—and not in circles."

"He knows how to do everything good," Sam murmured, just loud enough for Jane to make out. There was no resentment in those words, only what might have been a young boy's yearning to measure up to the successful man who had fathered him.

She thought about simply pretending she hadn't heard, and found she couldn't. "He doesn't know everything he needs to when it comes to fishing," she murmured back. "If you stick with it and don't give up, I'll teach you as much as I can today."

Sam said nothing, but the set of his jaw was enough. He appeared determined to hang in there.

And now it was her turn, Jane realized, to make good on her word. Fortunately, past experience made her confident enough in her abilities to deem her promise achievable. Too bad she was nowhere near as confident about being able to deal with the fact that three in a small boat would put her and her consultant in close contact. Maybe too close for comfort.

In a matter of minutes Adam took up the oars with practiced ease and whistled softly as he launched the weathered rowboat toward the middle of the lake with firm, sure strokes.

Okay, he could row, Jane had to admit. But she also had to wonder whether he'd be whistling so merry a tune on the way back.

"JUST GET THE damn—danged—hook out of my collar, will you?" Adam groused when the sun was well on its way to its noonday position high overhead. "I could do without having a slimy worm wiggling like crazy at the back of my neck."

Jane leaned in to inspect the problem, something she would have been glad to avoid since it put her in even closer proximity to the man she'd been doing her best to pay little attention to. It didn't help, not one bit, that for a startled moment she found her chest plastered to his back as the breeze ruffling the water suddenly picked up and rocked the boat under them.

She quickly tugged herself away. "I'll try to take care of it if you'll wait a double-darn minute for me to get the pliers from the tackle box," she huffed before dredging up a more patient tone. "I know it can't be all that comfortable, but I doubt the worm is having any more fun than you are."

That Adam had unwittingly stood up to stretch his legs just as she'd whipped Sam's short pole around to demonstrate how to drop a line into a shady spot was no one's fault. Reminding herself of that, she refused to feel guilty about catching the back of his collar with the sharp point of the hook.

"How come you said 'double darn'?" Sam asked as he joined her to peer into the dented metal box. "I never heard anybody say that before."

Jane reached in and retrieved the small pliers. "Sometimes one darn isn't enough," she explained. She didn't add that despite both her father and great-aunt having been known to swear like sailors, sometimes at each other, neither had ever accepted such language from a growing girl, and by the time that girl had become a woman, the habit of choosing alternatives had set in.

Leaving Sam sitting at one end of the boat, she straightened and turned toward the other end to go to Adam's aid. Unfortunately, she didn't get far. Instead, she stilled completely at the unexpected sight of a leanly muscled male chest.

And what a sight it was.

"You didn't have to take your shirt off," she said, meaning every word. Heaven knows that if he'd kept it on, she wouldn't be in danger of gawking at the broad expanse of bare skin with its swirls of dark hair.

"Easy for you to say," he groused yet again, handing her the shirt. "You didn't have a worm trying to get fresh with you."

Must be a female worm, she thought. Although she tried not to show it, she had to exert some effort to pull her gaze away from what her eyes stubbornly longed to roam over. After seating herself on a well-worn plank in the center of the boat, she used the pliers to snap off the tip of the hook, then untangled it from the stiff denim fabric that still held a trace of expensive cologne. That done, she handed the shirt back to Adam without so much as a glance in his direction.

By the time she'd put more bait on Sam's line and ventured another look at Adam, she found him seated with his shirt back on. "I'm casting again," she told him oh-so-politely.

"Thanks for the warning," he said, matching her tone.

At least he'd stopped grousing, she reflected as she went back to instructing Sam. When the boy landed his line in the shadow of the rocks after only a couple of failed attempts, Jane didn't hesitate to offer her praise. "Good job. Just let it sit there for a while and keep your eye on the bobber. If it disappears below the water, remember to jerk your line up to set the hook and then start reeling it in."

"Okay." Crouching, Sam propped his elbows on his knees and watched the red-striped plastic bobber.

Jane had been entertaining him on and off with stories of past fishing adventures, but now she sensed his need to concentrate and sat back. On her other side, Adam sent his line soaring out. Long minutes passed in silence broken only by the birds rustling in the trees. Then a fat fish popped straight out of the water near the end of Adam's line and landed with a huge splash.

"Wow!" Sam said.

"What the devil was that?" Adam asked in the next breath.

A smile flirted on Jane's mouth. "I'm betting that was Clever Clyde. He likes to let fishermen know he's out there, usually after he's just grabbed a worm off a hook right under their nose."

Adam cocked an eyebrow. "I suppose you mean under my nose."

Her smile didn't falter. "Could be."

He wasted no time in raising the hook out of the water—and there was no worm in sight. "The bobber didn't even move," he said in disgust.

Although she hadn't expected to, Jane was beginning to enjoy herself. "That's why they call him clever."

"Humph."

"Don't worry—I brought lots of worms," she assured him. Despite her struggle not to laugh, a chuckle spilled out. She tried to hide it with a cough, and knew she failed by the way his eyes narrowed— exactly as they had when he'd accepted her dare.

Just then Sam shouted again. "My bobber went down! I think I got something!"

Jane spun around. "Did you set the hook?"

"Yeah."

"Then reel it in, and remember to keep the line tight so you don't lose whatever's on there."

"Okay. Okay." Sam repeated the word like a litany as he brought his catch in.

Jane reached for the net, leaned over the boat and scooped up a wiggling fish. She couldn't help but be sorry to see that it was a small trout. Too small.

"I caught one!" Still obviously thrilled, Sam stared down at the end of his line with wide eyes.

"And you should be proud that you did," Jane told him in no uncertain terms. Then she bit her lip. "But…"

"But it's too little to keep, Sam," Adam finished, his voice more gentle than she had ever heard it.

Sam snapped his head up to look at his father. "You mean I hafta toss it back?"

"It would be the right thing to do," Adam said.

"I have to agree," Jane chimed in.

Sam switched his gaze to her. Sensing the battle the boy was waging inside himself, she suddenly wanted to reach out and hug him, just hug him. And didn't, of course. Her role was guide, instructor, and maybe down the road casual friend, if he would allow it.

"Then you better take it off the hook and it let

go,'' Sam told her at last in a small voice, his narrow shoulders drooping.

Jane accomplished that task with a few skillful movements and dropped the fish back into the lake. It swam off in the next instant. "You don't always have to let a fish go," she assured Sam. "And a first catch, whether you get to keep it or not, is worth celebrating."

"That's right." Adam was quick to second her. "We didn't eat any of the apple pie and whipped cream I brought, Sam. We can have that tonight after our spaghetti."

Sam nodded, but seemed little happier.

"Pie and whipped cream are a real treat," Jane found herself saying in another effort to cheer him up. "And you're lucky to be getting spaghetti, too." *Imported from Italy yet,* she added to herself, recalling the fancy groceries. "It sure sounds like a step up from the macaroni and cheese I plan on having tonight."

Unexpectedly, Sam perked up at that news. "You're making macaroni and cheese?"

"Mmm-hmm."

He hesitated. "Enough for more than just you?"

"Sam…" Adam's tone took on a warning note.

"But she's making *mac and cheese,*" he said, as though it was one of his favorites.

"Yes, and it's her dinner," Adam replied firmly. "We have our own food."

Jane knew he was right. What the resort's guests ate or didn't eat was no concern of hers, and vice versa. Still, she discovered she had little defense against the plaintive look in one little boy's eyes.

"If you'd like some macaroni and cheese, you're

welcome to it,'' she said before she could let any doubts about the wisdom of that offer sway her. ''I'm no hotshot chef, but I usually make plenty when I cook.''

Rather than accepting, as he plainly wanted to, Sam waited for his father's verdict, then shuffled his feet and waited some more before Adam spoke at last.

''How about if we share our food?'' His gaze met Jane's when she turned her head his way. ''If you want to bring your dinner to our cabin,'' he told her, ''I'll make what I was planning on, and we can all have pie for dessert.''

She hadn't expected that invitation. She'd only intended to give Sam a hefty helping to take back with him. But refusing would be rude. Not that she had a problem with being a long way from courteous when someone deserved it. However, that didn't apply here.

''All right,'' she finally agreed.

''Cool!'' Sam said. ''Way cool!'' For the first time within her hearing, his young voice was ripe with anticipation of what he obviously considered a real treat in store for him. Somehow, the sound charmed her. In its own way, she decided, it was as charming as his father's grin.

Not that Adam Lassiter was grinning now. In fact, something told Jane that he was as wary as she was of their spending the evening together. Why he might feel that way she had no clue. After all, she didn't have a charming grin. Heck, she didn't have a charming bone in her body.

Unlike her, he was in no danger of letting a physical attraction override his better judgment. No, she was the one who had to watch her step.

IT HAD TO BE A FLUKE, Adam told himself as he stirred his special pasta sauce while it simmered on the narrow electric range. There was no logical reason the memory of Jane Pitt's body plastered to his for a bare instant when the boat had rocked her off balance that morning should have nagged at him for the rest of the day. No logical reason at all.

Yes, he'd felt her small breasts pressed against his back, despite how quickly she'd pulled away, but discovering she had the standard female equipment hardly came as a surprise. And yes, he supposed his male sensors had automatically taken note of not only shape and size, but softness. Still, it didn't follow that the memory should refuse to fade.

Maybe it was the fact that she hadn't been wearing a bra.

Which shouldn't have surprised him, either, he'd decided once he had a chance to think about it. Glory Ridge's owner was a far cry from the sort of woman who wore lacy underwear—the sort who had always been his type up till now. He was a man who appreciated the feminine touches—the feel of silk and satin under his fingers, the whiff of an exotic perfume.

Jane Pitt was a long way—light-years, in fact—from exotic. Everything about her was rooted to the spot she called home, much as the pines were rooted in the same rocky ground. So why couldn't he forget how she'd felt against him?

It damn well had to be a fluke.

Footsteps sounded on the porch steps. Sam sprang

off one of the living-room chairs and opened the screen door. "Hi," he said, the short greeting as bright as his space-themed T-shirt.

"Hi yourself," Jane replied with a small smile as she walked in carrying a large glass baking dish covered with tin foil. "As you can see," she told Sam, "I made a lot."

Her smile faltered for a moment when she caught sight of Adam standing in the kitchen. He didn't miss the fact that when it reappeared, it seemed a bit forced.

"Should we put that in the oven to keep it warm?" he asked, his voice deliberately casual. Despite his offhand tone, he couldn't stop himself from sweeping an assessing look over the front of another of the checked cotton shirts she apparently favored. In the next instant, he yanked his gaze up to meet her eyes, and had to hope she hadn't noticed.

Jane took a few quick steps toward him. "If you'll get the oven door, I'll put the baking dish in." That soon accomplished, she set the temperature on low and glanced over at the bottle of wine Adam had opened and placed on the counter.

"I've been letting it breathe," he said.

She raised a brow. "Breathe?"

"Allowing a wine, especially a red, to rest after opening it helps to bring out the flavor."

"If you say so," she murmured with a slight shake of her head. "Never knew a beer that had to breathe."

Ignoring the hefty dose of irony in that statement, he draped the well-worn dish towel he'd been holding over one shoulder. "I'm afraid I don't have any beer, but you're welcome to join me in a glass of wine.'' His tone was as mild as he could make it. He'd already decided that the best way to handle the evening was to play the role of polite host—no matter what.

She shrugged. "Maybe I'll give it a try. Once you're sure it's done enough breathing, of course."

With what he considered admirable restraint, Adam again ignored that last comment and poured the wine—not into small, footed bowls of sparkling crystal, as he would have back at his condo, but into two juice glasses—the best alternative that an earlier investigation of the cabin's kitchen cabinets had produced. He handed one to her, then lifted his own.

"Here's to a successful business association," he said by way of a toast.

"Cheers," Jane replied. She took a sip, then held up her glass, regarding it with what appeared to be a new respect. "This isn't half bad."

Her jaw would probably drop like a stone if she knew what he'd paid for that bottle, Adam thought. After an appreciative swallow that primed his taste buds for the meal to come, he set his glass on the counter and went back to stirring his sauce.

"What's in that stuff?" Jane asked after a moment, leaning one jeans-clad hip against the counter.

"Fresh tomatoes, mushrooms, onions, garlic and a little basil. Rather than cooking the sauce for hours over a low heat, as some classic recipes call for, this one is simmered only long enough to blend the flavors."

"Smells…interesting." She paused for a beat. "I wasn't sure if you could really cook."

"I'll leave that for you to decide," Adam told her as he dropped a large handful of dried pasta into a pot of boiling water. "I've already made a salad. We'll be ready to eat in a couple of minutes."

True to his word, dinner was soon served, and Jane offered her judgment on his effort as they sat around the small kitchen table. "I can't say I've ever had spaghetti made exactly this way before, but it's pretty tasty."

"This mac and cheese is great," Sam said, giving his opinion of Jane's effort with a lopsided grin. He forked up another helping from a heaping plateful and swallowed it with an audible gulp. "You should have some, Dad."

Adam relished the sound of being called "Dad" for the second time in as many days. He couldn't help but view it as a small chink in the invisible wall his son had built up, even if Sam had turned the chance to try any of his father's contribution to their dinner down flat. *It wasn't you who put that boyish grin on your son's face, Lassiter,* he told himself. Still, much as he might have wished he'd been the one to accomplish that, he had to be grateful for the sight.

"There'll probably be plenty left for both of you to have for dinner tomorrow," Jane said. "I saved a plateful for myself before I brought it over," she added in the next breath, as though warding off the possibility that either of her companions might suggest she join them for leftovers.

"Mac and cheese two days in a row." Sam smacked his lips. "Boy, oh, boy."

"Then I'll leave sampling it until tomorrow," Adam said, equally content to avoid issuing another invitation to share a meal. Rather than joining in, he concentrated on his dinner and listened as Sam divided his attention between his food and their guest, who told him more stories about living in a place so unlike any he'd encountered during his young life.

"One of the best things about the nights out here is that you can see the stars," Jane said, forking up more pasta.

Sam lifted one thin shoulder in a shrug. "You can see the stars all over."

"Not as clearly as you can here. You may not have gotten a good look up at the sky last night, but it's true." Jane sipped her wine. "This time of year you don't even need a telescope to more than make out major constellations like the Northern Cross."

"I know about the Big Dipper and the Little Dipper." Sam took a break from eating and frowned in thought. "When it gets dark, can you show me how to find the cross?"

Jane hesitated. "It won't be dark for a while," she pointed out. "The sun's just going down." She glanced out the bare kitchen window, where a reddish glow lit the sky.

"You could stay until it gets dark," Sam suggested.

"Well..."

As Jane's voice drifted to a halt, Adam stepped in. "If our guest wants to go back to her cabin after dinner," he told his son, "it's her choice."

Sam nodded his agreement, but that didn't stop him from venturing another comment to Jane. "*Do* you want to go back? We still hafta have dessert," he reminded her. "Dad said I get to have two pieces 'cause I'm celebrating catching a fish."

She hesitated again, something stirring in her gaze, something that just might bear more than a passing resemblance to the caring warmth he had caught on the first day they'd met, Adam reflected. Back then, she'd been looking around at the old, run-down resort. This time, whatever her gaze held, it was directed squarely at his son.

"I suppose if you're going to have two pieces of that apple pie," she said at last, "it may be dark enough by the time we get finished."

"Awright!" Sam polished off his macaroni and cheese with one last swallow. "I'm ready for pie—*and* whipped cream," he declared in short order.

Getting through the cleanup didn't take long, despite the lack of a dishwasher. Then, at Jane's suggestion, they had their pie sitting on the porch steps. As the light gradually faded, Sweet Pea appeared through the trees and strolled by.

Jane tossed the skunk a piece of crust, which Sweet Pea first sniffed tentatively, then accepted with an eager gulp.

"Does she live in the woods?" Sam asked, wiping a last smear of whipped cream from his mouth as the skunk ambled away.

"Mostly she makes herself at home under the porch of my cabin," Jane replied. She set her empty plate on the side of the steps. "I think it's dark enough. Let's find an open spot where we can see off to the north."

"I'll take your plate," Adam told Sam, and stacked it on his own. While the adults had finished one slice of pie, the eight-year-old had wolfed down two with no trouble.

Adam watched as Jane led Sam several feet away and turned to what must have been north. Although he had to accept her word for that, he had no doubt she knew her directions. She pointed, his son nodded and then they both stared up into the distance. Within minutes Jane headed back to where Adam sat, leaving Sam to stand where he was, his attention fixed on the heavens.

"I should be going," she told Adam.

For some reason, he didn't urge her on her way—although it might be better all around if he did, he admitted. The last thing he needed was to start thinking about how her front had felt snug against his back—something he'd managed to avoid doing for a few hours. Far from encouraging her to stay, he would only be smart to let her go before his eyes were again tempted to wander to the gentle rise of her breasts.

Instead, smart or not, he found himself saying, "Might as well finish your wine."

Jane looked at the half-filled glass she'd set down on the porch steps when they'd first come out. "I guess I can," she said after a moment. Suiting action to words, she reseated herself on the top step and picked up her wine.

Adam stretched out his denim-clad legs and stacked one booted foot over the other. So what do you say now? he asked himself. In the end, he settled on the most reliable of neutral topics—the weather.

"Think it'll rain tomorrow?"

She shook her head. "We could use some, but I'm inclined to think that, contrary to the usual pattern, it'll be a while before the summer storms start up. When they do, they may make up for lost time, but until the clouds start regularly rolling in, nature should be providing a nightly show." She looked at Sam, who continued to study the flickering pinpoints of light crowding the sky. "Sometimes when I was a kid I used to get lost in the stars—just like Sam."

Lost in the stars. Yes, that would describe it, Adam had to agree, noting the rapt expression on his son's face, visible even in the dim glow of the porch light. "It seems he's found one thing about the great outdoors to fascinate him."

Hushed seconds passed before Jane spoke. "He didn't want to come here, did he?" she asked quietly.

Adam snapped his head her way and found her gaze waiting to meet his. "No," he acknowledged after another hushed moment, his voice as quiet as hers.

"It may be none of my business," she said, "but I can't help wondering why you brought him."

"I had my reasons," he told her. He intended to leave it at that, only to soon discover he couldn't.

"God knows, it wasn't to make him miserable," something compelled him to add, his voice still low enough to reach her ears alone, yet rock-solid firm, as well.

Her eyes remained steady on his. "I never thought any such thing, not for one minute. It's as clear as fresh spring water, at least it is to me, that you care about him—a lot."

Those words, still quiet yet somehow blunt enough to leave no question that she truly meant them, sliced through his considerable defenses and went straight to the core of him. This woman—this far-from-cold woman who could put up a hard front, yet seemed to have a soft spot in her heart where his son was concerned—had touched a place inside him few people had before her. Despite his resolve to keep his personal feelings private, he responded with equal bluntness before he'd thought twice about it.

"Yes, I care. I care one hell of a lot. That's why I want my son back."

Chapter Four

He wanted his son back.

Puzzled, Jane searched for a possible explanation as silent seconds passed. She was still mulling the matter over when Sam gave up on his stargazing and walked back to the cabin.

"I found the Little and Big Dipper, too," he told her. "They seem brighter out here. I never saw the moon look so big, either."

She smiled immediately, automatically responding to the unmistakable wonder in his young voice. "Amazing what you can see with no city lights around to compete with the view, hmm?"

"Uh-huh." Sam agreed with a sudden yawn wide enough to display a mouthful of small white teeth.

"I think it's about bedtime for you," Adam remarked in short order. "It may still be early, but considering that we all got up before dawn, it's already been a long day."

Looking sleepier by the minute, Sam didn't argue the point. He said his good-nights, and the screen door soon closed behind him as he went inside.

Jane traded another look with the man seated just inches away. She had a hunch he might be regretting what he'd told her minutes earlier. Which didn't mean her curiosity, now roused, was ready to conveniently fade.

"Since Sam is with you for the summer, why would you say you want him back?" she asked, her voice again soft in the quiet around them.

He hesitated, as though debating how, or maybe even whether, to reply. "Sam may be with me now," he said at last, "but things aren't the same as they used to be between us. There was the divorce, of course—and, more recently, his mother's remarriage. When he arrived for the summer this year and I saw how wary he was about our spending time together, it really hit me how much he and I have grown apart. Living on opposite sides of the country for most of the year seems to have taken its toll."

And that worried him, she thought, noting his abruptly sober expression.

"So you brought him here to fix the situation," she ventured with a lifted brow.

"Yes," he replied after another silent moment, and left it at that.

Jane ran her tongue around her teeth. "Well, the two of you probably agreed on at least one thing this morning."

He batted a pesky mosquito away with a large hand as his mouth slanted wryly. "If you're suggesting that we were both a lot less than thrilled at the prospect of stumbling out of bed before the birds were even up, you're correct."

His rueful admission only confirmed what she'd already suspected; neither father nor son was an early riser. "Look on the bright side, though," she said. "You probably got the chance to grumble together."

He shook his head slowly. "There, you would be wrong. Sam got to grumble. I had to maintain an upbeat tone and keep my griping to myself."

She swallowed an urge to chuckle. "Must have been tough."

"Damn right." He heaved a gusty breath. "And then, once we were finally awake enough to notice, we didn't even catch any fish worth keeping."

"*You* didn't catch any—period," she couldn't help but point out, recalling that he'd lost more than one worm to Clever Clyde before they'd called it a day.

"Don't remind me."

Despite the small—and somewhat smug, she admitted—pleasure that jogging his memory undeniably gave her, Jane was ready to let the subject drop, until she remembered something else.

He knows how to do everything good, Sam had said about his father. It probably hadn't hurt, she decided, that the man in question had proved otherwise that day.

"Could be it was a plus for Sam that he was the one who caught a fish, little as it was," she said. "When a man with a growing son is successful at most everything he does, it might not be a bad notion to let a less-confident side of himself show now and then."

He batted away another mosquito, then angled his head and considered her words. "Do you ever let a less-confident side of yourself show?" he asked.

Although she supposed it was a fair question, Jane found herself skirting it. "Unlike you, I don't have a growing child in the picture," she said. Sitting forward, she propped her elbows on her knees. "I've got the feeling he looks up to you, you know, just like I have the feeling you were proud of him for not putting up a fuss about tossing that little trout back."

"I *was* proud of him," Adam told her, this time without hesitation. "I've always been proud of him."

"Good," she replied just as readily. "It's a lucky kid who has a proud father on the family tree."

Again he turned the tables on her, swiftly and smoothly taking the conversation into her territory. "Is your father proud of you?"

She raised her glass for a short sip. He couldn't know how that particular question would sting, even now. "My father's not around anymore. He was killed in a ranching accident a while back." Jane forged on before any condolences could be offered. "My four elder brothers were long gone by the time it happened and I'd already settled in here, so my sister and her husband took over the Pitt ranch." And turned the sadly neglected place into somewhere worth living, she added to herself.

"Do you have any sisters or brothers?" she asked, once more shifting subjects.

"No brothers. One older sister who lives in Europe. She married a Brit and helps him run a business in London."

A sister in England. Parents in Scottsdale. An ex-wife in Boston who was probably a blue-blood by birth.

The more she learned about him, the more that knowledge emphasized the differences between her and this man, Jane mused. Not that she hadn't been aware of them from the minute she'd laid eyes on him. She had. Anyone who got even a passing look would probably label the two of them total opposites.

Which, she assured herself, was fine with her.

Jane polished off her wine with a last swallow, set down her glass and rose to her feet. "I need to go," she said in no uncertain terms, determined to stick to her guns this time.

Adam stood, as well, and batted away yet another mosquito that buzzed right past his nose. "Why are they plaguing me and leaving you alone?" he groused.

The chuckle she'd held back earlier broke from her throat, a low, rich sound. "It's your fancy cologne, Slick," she said dryly, heading down the steps and off into the night before he could do more than mutter a curse.

"See you tomorrow," she called out, aiming the words over her shoulder.

"Not at the crack of dawn," he called back.

No, not tomorrow, she thought as she continued on her way. But they'd be going fishing again. Maybe Adam hadn't caught the fever…but his son had. She knew the signs. Sam would soon be eager to try his luck, and because his father seemed determined that they spend time together, they'd both wind up with poles in hand before too long. She was sure of it.

What she was a lot less certain of was how things would all work out in the end with her two current guests. Would Adam get his son back, as he'd phrased it? Somehow, although it really was none of her concern, she had to hope so.

Jane sighed a small sigh. She also had to hope and pray that she would get what she wanted, that her

hotshot consultant would come through and Glory
Ridge Resort would once again be a thriving operation.

But is that all you want? an inner voice whispered
in her ear. *Or, after coming up against a man you're
drawn to despite yourself, do you want something
more?*

Do you want…him?

She tossed her head in an effort shake off that
question—the last question she had any desire to
dwell on. Nonetheless, it dogged her footsteps all the
way back to Pitt's Pride.

By the time she'd spent a restless night caught up
in vivid images of things she had no business imagining, Jane was ready to strangle Adam Lassiter.

"I THINK SOMEONE woke up on the wrong side of
the bed this morning."

Adam offered that remark after Jane had closed
yet another file cabinet drawer with a near slam. He'd
always considered himself too smart ever to contend
that he had a true understanding of the female half
of the population, but he knew a ticked-off woman
when he saw one.

"At least I got up at a decent hour," she muttered
darkly.

He also recognized a dig when he heard it. He
wasn't inclined to let it go, either.

"I didn't realize I was on a time clock," he said,
leaning back in his swivel chair.

She stared down at him for a second, then made
a clear effort to rein in her temper. "You're not.
Forget I mentioned it."

"Uh-huh."

He returned his gaze to the computer screen and

went back to his research. He had to admit to being surprised by the number of facilities that catered to the outdoor crowd. Some targeted just one or two segments of the market, he'd noted. Others, as the Web site he was currently visiting demonstrated, took on the whole spectrum, and did it with style.

Adam sat forward as a quick click of the pointer started an online tour of a cabin far larger, and light-years newer, than any at Glory Ridge. "You could throw a dinner party in this place," he murmured after a moment.

Jane stepped up behind him to look over his shoulder. "Holy Toledo. They're calling that a *cabin?*"

"Indeed they are."

She snorted. "With six bedrooms? Looks more like a motel to me."

Catching the underlying defensiveness in that last comment, he couldn't resist the urge to jerk her chain, just a little. "I think the spiral staircase up to the loft off the living room is a particularly nice touch."

She issued another snort. "Seems to me people would get dizzy going around in circles."

"Oh, I think they'd manage," Adam said.

Ignoring that dry remark, Jane walked around the desk and sat down across from him. "Well, maybe we don't have fancy staircases at Glory Ridge," she said, placing a thick ledger book on the card table she'd set up, "but we do have a customer. I got a call earlier this morning from a guy who wants to park his RV in the campground for what could be as long as a month. He's supposed to show up late next week."

Adam didn't bother to point out that one customer

would hardly add up to much profit on the resort's bottom line. They both knew it. Instead, he watched as she opened the ledger, picked up an old ballpoint pen and began to write with quick, bold strokes.

"Is that by any chance the guest register?" he inquired.

"Mmm-hmm." Jane kept on writing, reading off a scratch pad by the phone. "I enter the names and dates as people ask for reservations, then fill in the rest of their info when they get here."

Given his companion's chancy mood, he debated whether to risk a rebuff, then said, "You know, a computer could be programmed to keep track of that kind of information." Not to mention other programs that could be used for a host of things, he thought, such as keeping the resort's financial records. "It might be a wise investment."

She glanced up. "I wouldn't say no to getting one."

So she had the good sense not to scoff at all modern conveniences. Pleased to discover as much, he inclined his head in a brisk nod of approval.

What he didn't do was confidently contend that business was sure to pick up enough to justify the expense, because the matter remained in doubt. So far, his research showed that the resort faced some stiff competition. But it was too early to make any judgments. He still had a ways to go to complete an in-depth market analysis.

Jane tossed the pen on the table and closed the ledger. "What's Sam up to?"

"Last time I saw him, he was drawing a map of the stars he identified last night. He's already given me a few broad hints on what a good idea ordering a telescope online and shipping it to Glory Ridge would be.''

A smile played around her mouth, the first he'd seen that day. "Something tells me one will show up before too long."

Was he that transparent? After last evening, when he'd revealed more than he'd intended to about his relationship with his son, Adam supposed he just might be. "I plan to take a look at some before I sign off," he admitted.

Footsteps in the outer room drew his attention to the doorway. Seconds later Sam appeared, with a boy around his age following a step behind. The new arrival had a thick thatch of russet hair, a smattering of freckles across his small, upturned nose and a glint of mischief in his cagey green eyes.

Jane introduced the boy to Adam as her nephew, Travis Malloy.

"Hi," Travis offered with a friendly grin that showed teeth shades brighter than his well-worn white T-shirt.

"I guess you and Sam have already met," she said, glancing from one boy to the other.

"Yeah." Travis stuffed his hands into the pockets of jeans every bit as battered as those his aunt favored. "I never met anybody from Boston before."

"It was a first for me, too," Jane acknowledged.

That news hardly surprised Adam. He doubted many people from that venerable old city travelled clear across the country to visit a place so easy to overlook. One thing for sure, he couldn't even imagine Ariel and her new husband, who apparently came from a long line of prominent East Coast bankers, making the trek.

Then again, just weeks earlier he would never have imagined himself making the trek. And here he was.

"Travis came on his bike from his house on the other side of the mountain," Sam explained to his father. "I bet it's nice having a bike to ride up here," he added much too casually.

"A guy's gotta have wheels," Travis said, as though it were a given.

"Yeah." Sam nodded a mile a minute in response. "Wheels are good."

Jane bit back a smile and waited to see if Adam would agree. That Sam had meant it would be nice if *he* had a bike to ride while he was at Glory Ridge had to be as clear to Adam as it was to her.

"You've got a bike at home," Adam pointed out, matching his son's casual tone.

So, as much as he cared about his only child, he wasn't a pushover when it came to buying things left and right. Even though Jane had little doubt Adam could afford to be indulgent, she had to admire his restraint.

"If you don't mind one that doesn't have all the bells and whistles," she told Sam, "I've still got the bike I rode up and down the trails around here when I was a kid. You could use it while you're here. It's old, but it's still in fairly good shape."

Sam frowned as he mulled over the offer. "Wouldn't it be a girl's bike?"

Travis responded by giving his head a decisive shake. "My Aunt Jane wouldn't pick out a *girl's* bike," he contended, both with assurance and more than a hint of pride in his relative, as though he be-

lieved she had little regard for "girl things" and admired her for it.

"Actually, I didn't choose the bike," Jane said.
"It was a hand-me-down from one of my brothers.
But I was happy enough with it, I'll admit."

Flashing a satisfied grin, Travis said, "You didn't
play with dolls, either, did you?"

"I left that to your mother," she acknowledged.
Ellen always got dolls for presents, Jane remembered. Plus a brand-new bicycle on one occasion. A
girl's model, of course.

"This would be an older sister of yours?" Adam
asked.

"No, my younger—and only, as it happens."

When a dark eyebrow winged up at that news,
Jane had no trouble crediting his surprise to her
nephew's age. "Ellen married Mitch Malloy shortly
after they both graduated from Harmony High," she
said. "Travis was born less than a year later." Once
again she fixed her attention on Sam. "So, do you
want to borrow the bike?"

He glanced at his father. At Adam's nod, giving
the go-ahead, he seemed to accept the fact that a new
one wasn't in his future. "I guess so."

"Why don't you and Sam check it out," Jane told
her nephew. "It's in the shed behind Pitt's Pride.
Door's open."

After the boys trooped out, their small feet slap-
ping on the bare wood floor, Adam looked at Jane.
"Thanks."

She shrugged. "No problem. A bike really is a
handy thing for a kid to have up here, and you don't
have to worry about him if he's riding around with

Travis. They won't get lost." *Not like a city-raised father and son might if they went off by themselves.*

Although she'd kept that last reflection to herself, his next statement quickly countered it. "I don't plan on getting lost while I'm here, either."

So he'd said before, shortly after he and Sam had arrived at Glory Ridge, as she recalled. She didn't point out that they had yet to put those backpacks with the store tags still on them to good use on a hiking expedition.

"Mmm-hmm," she offered in a strictly neutral response.

Just then, the cell phone hooked on Adam's tooled-leather belt rang. The conversation that followed featured phrases like "prime market penetration" and "consumer demographics."

Most of it sounded like a foreign language to Jane. Still, she had no trouble recognizing that her consultant knew what he was talking about. Despite his relaxed pose as he lounged back in his seat, quiet confidence rumbled through his deep voice.

The same voice she'd imagined whispering intimate suggestions in her ear during a long and anything but restful night, one of which had been—

With a short, silent oath, Jane yanked her attention back to where it belonged. Tonight, she vowed, she wouldn't have any thoughts, intimate or otherwise, about the man who still looked out of his element in his too-new denim. Unfortunately for her peace of mind, he also still looked all too attractive in spite of it.

"Remember," he said into the phone, "you're poised to have one of the hot gifts of the Christmas season, so don't worry about the advertising budget.

Spend what's needed to get the word out there in a big way, and the profit on your bottom line will have you doing a merry jig by New Year's.'' With that last reassurance, he disconnected.

''Mind if I ask what the hot gift is?'' Jane's curiosity had her saying.

''A glow-in-the-dark vibrator.''

Mystified by that information, Jane frowned. ''You're kidding. Why in the world would anyone want to be able to see something like that in the…''

She halted, all at once getting more than a clue what he was talking about. She'd read an article on ''personal'' vibrators in a women's magazine at Cuts 'N Curls. Not that there'd been any mention of them glowing in the dark! Despite her determination to appear not in the least shocked, she felt her cheeks warm with the beginnings of a blush.

Good grief, she never blushed!

His smile widened in a way that said he'd noticed. Oh, yes. He had.

''It's being packaged for the strictly adult market, of course,'' he told her, his gray eyes glinting with frank amusement.

''I should hope so,'' she huffed. ''It's no toy for kids, that's for sure.''

''No,'' he agreed.

His smile gradually faded as an inquisitive spark lit in his gaze. ''Speaking of toys, though, why didn't you ever want to play with dolls?''

He didn't have it quite right, but she saw no need to correct him. Instead, Jane raised one shoulder in an offhand shrug, assuming the subject would be dropped if she said nothing.

"Or did you want to at one time," he went on, "and never got any to play with?"

So he wasn't only intelligent but perceptive. Still, she wasn't about to confess that even her mother had never thought of giving the elder Pitt daughter, the "tomboy" in the family, a doll. Then again, Jane thought, her pesky brothers would probably have razzed her to death if she'd taken to putting frilly dresses on dolls.

Only Ellen, the youngest and undeniably the most sweet-natured of the Pitt clan, could get away with something like that. She'd been able to wrap them all, sometimes even the gruff male who ruled over the household, around her delicate little finger.

"One way or the other, the days of playing with dolls are long behind me," Jane said.

Rather than pointing out that she hadn't really answered his question, he let the subject drop and went back to his research. "Five-star mattresses," he murmured after a moment, his gaze again locked on the computer screen.

Lounging back in her chair, she silently counted to ten, then to twenty, before her curiosity got the upper hand yet again. "What about mattresses?"

"The place with the spiral staircase gives theirs a five-star rating."

She knew better than to ask how many he'd give the one he was currently sleeping on at Squirrel Hollow. "Sounds like a movie review to me," she scoffed.

"If it wins customers, it's a good pitch. That's the first law of promotion."

Promotion was all well and good, she had to allow,

but it had its limits. "There was a time when a vacation in the woods was about roughing it."

As he glanced up to meet her gaze, his smile made a swift return. "I guess these days some people would rather rough it on a world-class mattress."

People like you.

Although she didn't voice that thought, the words seemed to hover over the quiet room. As if he'd heard them loud and clear, he added, "And maybe you shouldn't judge top-of-the-line mattresses before you've bounced on one."

She lifted her chin a short notch. "Which you have, of course. And not alone, I'm sure." That last statement left her lips before she even considered the wisdom of taking the conversation into such private territory. And now it was too late to take it back.

"Not that it's any of my business," she hastened to say, straightening in her seat.

"No, it's not," he acknowledged far too courteously. "But for the record, I haven't bounced on a mattress, top-of-the-line or otherwise, with anyone lately." He paused for a beat. "How about you?"

There was no point in snarling at him, she told herself. She was the one who'd started this. Her only option was to finish the matter as quickly as possible.

"Me, neither," she muttered.

He raised a brow. "No...bouncing?"

"None," she said through clenched teeth, and with that she hopped to her feet, grabbed up the ledger and stomped across the room to replace it in a top cabinet drawer. She did her best not to hear Adam's deep chuckle. And heard it anyway.

It was the same wicked-around-the-edges sound she'd imagined more than once the night before. The

same sound that w
voice that had whisp
ear. The same sound
couldn't.

Jane didn't slam the
time.

But she wanted to.

Chapter Five

"Never thought I'd see you decked out in denim—
and not the designer stuff, either—at this time in your
life, cuz." Ross Hayward's eyes, almost the same
shade of deep navy as his well-tailored suit, sparkled
with wry humor as he faced Adam across a red-vinyl
booth at Dewitt's Diner.

The diner had been a fixture in downtown Harmony for over fifty years and was reputed never to
have done less than a brisk business at lunchtime.
Adam had no trouble recalling a point in his own
past when he and his Hayward cousin had occupied
a pair of the chrome-legged stools facing a wide window at the front of the restaurant, staring out at pas-
sersby while relishing one of Dewitt's trademark
chocolate malts.

Just as his son and Travis Malloy were doing now,
Adam noted. The boys, well on their way to becoming friends, had already woofed down their meal, after which Sam had declared Dewitt's to be his new
favorite spot to indulge in a thick, juicy hamburger
along with a sizzling stack of crisp fries.

His own stomach comfortably full, Adam considered the merits of just relaxing to the mellow ballad

drifting from the classic jukebox that was as much a part of Dewitt's as its popular soda fountain. The truth was, he wouldn't have thought twice about leaning back in his seat and doing exactly that—*if* his companion hadn't appeared quite so amused.

"Why am I getting the feeling that you're delighted to be laughing at my expense?" he asked dryly.

"Probably because I am," Ross admitted with cheerful candor. He ran a long finger down his tall glass of iced cola. "Has Mother Nature whipped you into shape yet?"

Adam propped his elbows on the table, thinking that he could have done without the current conversational turn. He and Ross had spent the better part of lunch catching up on family news, and he was pleased to see that his cousin seemed happier since remarrying the previous year. In fact, with two beautiful blond daughters from his first marriage, a new strikingly attractive brunette wife and a baby they'd recently learned was on the way, Ross looked like a very satisfied man these days, and Adam could only be glad.

He would have been even more glad if the person he'd considered his best pal before the Lassiters had relocated to the Phoenix area when he was ten years old didn't seem determined to take the discussion into new territory—at his expense, of course.

"If you mean, have I become an avid fan of getting up before dawn to plop a fishing line in the water," Adam said at length, "the answer is no."

But his son was another story, he had to concede. During the past several days, Sam had voted to go fishing more than once—with no complaints about facing the day while it was still dark. Then again, the boy had actually managed to reel in a trout big enough to keep his second time out.

"Would I be safe in assuming that you haven't caught anything?" Ross asked. Again his amusement was plain.

Adam released a long breath. Sam had already passed along the news of his accomplishment, going so far as to offer an eager, blow-by-blow description of the whole thing. But, with surprising diplomacy for one so young, he hadn't mentioned his father's failure to duplicate his achievement. A failure that stuck in Adam's craw, he couldn't deny.

"Haven't caught a thing," he acknowledged in the mildest tone he could muster.

So far, Clever Clyde—and what the hell kind of name was that for a fish, anyway?—had zeroed in without warning and stolen more bait. After which, the fat trout had jumped high and hit the water with enough force to ensure he got credit for his thieving ways.

Someday, Adam vowed. *Someday I'll haul the bastard in and see him wiggling on the end of my line.*

A smile played around Ross's mouth as he ventured another question. "What do you think of Glory Ridge's owner?"

Adam didn't have to spend any time considering that one. "I think she's a force to be reckoned with," he said. "Thanks," he added with a hefty dose of irony, "for aiming her my way."

Ross lifted a hand and ran it through his hair. That hair, a rich golden brown, had been skillfully cut—not at a salon that catered to both sexes, Adam more than suspected, but at the local barbershop, a long-standing tradition in Harmony's male community. This was a place where tradition, going back to the founders who had first settled the area, took precedence.

"All I did was recommend you. You didn't have to take the job," Ross reminded him. "Sorry you did?"

Adam knew he could hardly regret his decision when the gap between him and his only child was closing. It wasn't happening quickly, not by any means, but he now heard the word "Dad" regularly from Sam's lips, just as had once been routine, and he had to be grateful. He would never, he thought, take it for granted again.

"No, I'm not sorry," he said. "Even if," he couldn't resist tacking on, "the woman and I seem to rub each other the wrong way more often than not."

"I'm guessing the woman is Jane Pitt," a low voice, coming from beside the booth, abruptly drawled.

After a swift turn of his head, Adam had no trouble recognizing who that voice belonged to. He and Tom Kennedy, Harmony's veteran police chief, had renewed their acquaintance less than a year earlier at Ross's wedding. For that occasion, Tom, who favored Western shirts paired with casual pants and a wide-brimmed cowboy hat, had worn a suit. Today, Adam noted, the police chief, a sturdily built man on the far side of sixty, was once again decked out in his typical garb.

"You're right about the woman in question," Ross informed the new arrival.

That Ross didn't ask how Tom had managed to guess correctly came as no surprise to Adam. Ross, having lived in Harmony all his life, was sure to know even better than Adam did how fast news got around in a small city. By now, many residents were probably aware that Jane Pitt had hired herself a business consultant who was no stranger to at least some of them.

Tom reached up and thumbed back his hat. "Mind if I join you gentlemen?"

"Not at all," Adam said even as Ross slid over to make space on his side of the booth.

Tom was barely seated when a young waitress sporting a long blond ponytail appeared to take his order. He opted for coffee and a slice of cherry pie.

"With a scoop of peppermint ice cream on the side?" she asked.

He grinned. "You've got my number, Cindy."

The waitress left, then returned in record time with Tom's coffee. He took a long sip and studied Adam over the brim of his mug. "So you and Jane Pitt aren't seeing eye to eye."

"Not always," Adam acknowledged. A prime example was that day in the office when a short conversation about personal vibrators had put a soft blush on her cheeks. A flattering blush, he had to concede.

Flattering enough, in fact, to have him forgetting who they both were for an instant while he'd wondered how her small, bare mouth would taste under his.

All too soon, though, that blush had faded, replaced by her clear displeasure—with him.

Tom set his mug down. "As a lifelong bachelor,

I can't lay claim to being any sort of authority on women, but from what I've seen of the Pitt clan over the years, I'd say the older girl in that family didn't have it easy growing up.''

Adam scooped up a last fry from his plate. "If that's true, I suppose it might explain a few things."

Nodding, Tom said, "Like why she's developed a reputation for giving a whole new meaning to the words *independent female*."

"Cripes, she's independent, all right," Adam muttered.

"I'm betting she had to be to cope with a pack of brothers who didn't care much about family ties. They sure didn't stick around once they were old enough to make their own way." Tom's expression turned thoughtful. "Then again, maybe if I'd had Owen Pitt for a father, I would've left as soon as I could, too."

That caught Adam's attention. Given that he and Jane had to deal with each other, he imagined his curiosity was only natural. "The guy wasn't exactly the ideal parent, huh?"

"Not hardly." Tom's pie was served. He forked up a bite as the waitress left, then hummed his approval as he swallowed. "The only person Pitt had a soft spot in his hard heart for was Ellen, the youngest child. He didn't come into town much, seemed to prefer keeping himself and his family out at their ranch. But I remember years ago watching him drive up Main Street with the two girls in his old pickup. They were small enough to need helping out of the truck, and he handed Jane down like a sack of beans he couldn't wait to unload. When it was Ellen's turn, though, he treated her like a fragile china doll. And she was as pretty as a little doll, I have to admit. Then he took his younger daughter's hand and left the older girl to trail behind them—as they walked down the sidewalk.''

Tom's mouth thinned in disgust. "He never even glanced back to see if she was following, but I saw her shoulders droop for a second before she squared them and started marching right behind.''

"Sounds like he was a real jackass," Ross remarked, his tone revealing his own disgust.

"Indeed it does," Adam had to agree.

He also had to wonder if a good bit of who Jane Pitt was now didn't hark back to that child who'd been left to tag along. Interesting, he thought.

Tom ate more pie. "Hear you're taking a vacation," he said with a sidelong look at Ross.

"As usual, Harmony's grapevine has it right," Ross replied. "Jenna and I are going to the West Coast with the kids for a few weeks. We're leaving next Monday.''

Having already been filled in on his cousin's plans, Adam had agreed to drive Sam over to the Hayward house for Sunday dinner before Ross and his family left. *One meal I don't have to cook,* Adam reflected. He and his son might be slowly bridging that gap, but Sam still displayed little enthusiasm for his father's culinary creations. Maybe he should ask Jane for her macaroni and cheese recipe. Oh, yeah. She'd probably be damn pleased to have that to lord over him.

"And if I'm taking a vacation, I'd better get back to work soon," Ross went on, brushing a stray piece of lint from his striped silk tie. "My lunch hour has already turned into two, and there's a Harmony Business Council meeting I have to attend this evening. Word is that a plan to promote businesses in the area is being proposed.''

''Most do pretty well now,'' Tom commented. ''Especially in the summer with the tourist season in full force.''

''Still, a bit of the right kind of promotion never hurts,'' Ross contended.

''Couldn't have said it better,'' Adam agreed.

Tom included both cousins in a sweeping glance. ''Spoken like two sharp businessmen. Even if,'' he continued with a sly look at Adam, ''you don't precisely resemble one today.''

Adam didn't ask what he did resemble. In the police chief's eyes, it wouldn't be a seasoned outdoorsman, he was sure. Maybe the denim he wore wasn't quite so new or stiff, maybe his boots no longer held a polished gleam, but he still would have felt more at home wearing a suit. And, more than likely, it showed.

Tom polished off his pie. ''I've got to get going, too.'' He took a last sip of his coffee and signaled for his check.

''My treat,'' Adam told the older man, picking up the luncheon check the waitress had already left. ''That goes for you, too, cuz,'' he added to Ross.

''Thanks.'' Again Ross's gaze lit with amusement. ''I figured you'd spring for the meal, considering what you consultant types usually get paid.''

He wasn't getting paid at all for his current job, Adam could have countered. Then again, this might be one instance where his efforts could fail to produce the usual results. The more research he did, the more apparent it became that Glory Ridge faced a far-from-enviable future. He hadn't shared those findings with Jane yet, but he knew he would have to, and soon.

Tom rubbed his well-padded stomach, then slid out of the booth and waited while Ross followed suit. "Think your relative is trying to make up for the times I let him off the hook, like the day he snuck out of the house with a pair of scissors and snipped a bunch of fur off Mrs. Morrison's prized poodle?"

Ross lifted one broad shoulder in a shrug. "Could be. He did get into trouble now and then as a growing boy, didn't he?"

Tom gave Adam another sly look. "Tried to bluff his way through it, too. And mostly succeeded. As I recall, his story was that the poodle looked so hot with all that fur, he felt sorry for the poor thing."

Adam noticed that the chief made no mention of Ross getting into trouble. Probably because he hadn't. No, even as a child Ross had taken his standing as a member of one of Harmony's founding families seriously. It had been up to Adam to occasionally test the limits of how far a kid could go and still talk his way out.

"When your back's against the wall, act as innocent as an angel was my motto," he readily confessed before laughing right along with his companions. Still, he was glad that Sam, who was approaching with quick steps and Travis at his side, had been too far away to catch the reference to his father's misdeeds.

Adam introduced Sam to the police chief, and after a short conversation, Tom and Ross departed, Ross with a reminder that he'd see the Lassiters on Sunday.

"Time we took off," Adam told the boys.

Travis shoved his hands into his jean pockets. "Wanna stop at the place where my mom fixes hair and stuff? It smells funny there sometimes," he went on in an aside to Sam, "but it's not too bad if you hold your nose."

Adam had already met the boy's father when he and Sam had picked Travis up at the former Pitt place, which was now being worked by Mitch Malloy. Malloy struck him as a nice guy who'd taken on a big load and seemed to be succeeding at the ranching business, if on a small scale. How would Ellen, the youngest of the Pitts, strike him? Adam found he was far from opposed to discovering the answer to that question.

"Yes, I'd like to meet your mother," he said. He slid out of the booth. "We also need to do some grocery shopping."

Sam whipped out his tongue and swiped a smear of chocolate malt from a corner of his mouth. "I'm too full to eat."

"You'll be hungry again by dinnertime," Adam said with confidence as they walked toward the old-fashioned cash register stationed at the front of the diner.

"What are you guys having?" Travis wanted to know.

"Probably some broiled chicken breasts topped with sautéed mushrooms," Adam replied. After a lunch that could only be described as hearty, he was thinking of something fairly low fat.

Sam's face fell. Then his expression brightened in the next breath. "Maybe you could have that, and I could have…"

"Have what?" Adam prompted at his son's hesitation.

"I just remembered what Jane said to me this morning. When I told her we were going to this diner for lunch,· she said she liked the hamburgers they make here, but she liked what she was making tonight even better."

Adam halted in his tracks. "Sam, we're not imposing on Jane to share another of her meals with us."

Sam craned his neck back and gave his father a frankly pleading look. "But I bet she'd let me have some if you said it was okay, and what she's making is way better than chicken. It's even better than *steak*."

Adam's sigh was long and heartfelt. He had a hunch he was going to regret asking, and asked anyway. "And what's that?"

"Hot dogs, Dad!"

THE PHONE RANG just as Jane was about to close up the office and do some routine maintenance work. Regardless of how few guests were at the resort, the grass around the cabins had to be mowed and weeds always needed to be pulled. Since the weeding was one of her least favorite chores, Jane wasn't opposed to a reprieve in the form of answering the phone. It might even be someone wanting to make a reservation.

But she heard her sister's soft voice when she picked up the receiver on the second ring. "You'll never guess who just left Cuts 'N Curls."

"Male or female?"

"Oh, most definitely male. And tall, dark and gorgeous at that."

One particular male immediately popped into Jane's head. But she wasn't saying so. "Hmm. It would be hard to choose, what with all the tall, dark and gorgeous men in Harmony. They're lounging on practically every street corner."

Ellen laughed. "You don't fool me, sis. You know darn well I'm talking about Adam Lassiter. I figured that being related to the Haywards, he'd be attractive, but I didn't expect he'd be flashing a downright devastating grin to go with those good looks."

So he'd turned on the charm, had he? Jane reflected with a rueful slant of her lips. She supposed that many men would have felt at least a bit uncomfortable in a spot so patently geared to the female of the species. But obviously not her consultant. He'd probably blazed a trail right through the beauty shop while avid eyes followed his every move.

"He had hearts fluttering all over the place here," Ellen said, confirming Jane's suspicions. "Including, I have to admit, mine." Ellen paused for a beat. "You might have warned me that he was a dreamboat."

A *dreamboat?* Jane grimaced. "You're sounding like a moonstruck teenager, little sister. He's not that impressive."

"The heck he's not."

"Well, he hasn't fluttered my heart." She wasn't mentioning her pulse. Or how she'd felt at the sight of a bare-chested Adam.

"He may get to you yet," Ellen said. "And his son is certainly appealing, too, in his own way."

There, Jane had to agree. "He's a great kid. He

was a little lost when he got here, but he seems to be settling in.''

"He told everyone in the shop about the big fish he caught.''

It was Jane's turn to laugh. "It was big enough to keep, anyway. I don't think I've ever seen anyone so excited. I'd barely netted the thing when he started jumping up and down right in the boat. He could hardly wait until we got back so he could run for his camera and take a picture. Then I asked him if he was going to eat it, and he appeared thunderstruck at the idea. I believe his father dined alone on that trout.''

She'd had to give Adam a hasty lesson on how to scale and gut a fish, Jane recalled. To his credit, he'd done a passable job of it, even if he still hadn't caught any fish of his own.

Served him right, Jane thought when the phone conversation abruptly ended as Ellen was called away. The stubborn man continued to refuse to ask for help.

But that wasn't what had been troubling him lately. Something was, she more than suspected, but not a lack of fish on his line. More likely it had something to do with the job that had brought him here.

Something to do with Glory Ridge. So far, he hadn't said much, and she hadn't pressed him, but...

A shiver of unease ran down Jane's spine as every instinct she had told her to brace herself for bad news.

"THANKS FOR THE INFO, Phil. I appreciate it.''

Adam disconnected the call and hooked his phone back on his belt. After eating a solitary dinner while

Sam joined Jane for hot dogs cooked on an old charcoal grill she kept down by the lake, he had returned to the resort office and called a stockbroker acquaintance of his who specialized in the travel industry. Luckily, he'd been able to catch Phil on a short break between business trips.

Now, with the last-minute—and, as usual, insightful—information the stockbroker had offered, his research was finished. He just wished the results he couldn't avoid passing along to Jane were more to his liking.

As if his thoughts had summoned her, she appeared in the doorway to the office. Behind her, the outer room was dark, testifying that the sun had set.

"I left Sam back on the porch at Squirrel Hollow watching the sky through his new telescope," she told Adam. "He let me have a peek. It's pretty snazzy."

Adam leaned back in his chair. "He's getting such a kick out of it it was worth having it shipped here."

"I'd say you're right." Jane walked over and took the chair opposite him. "I expected to find you with your nose buried in the computer."

He tapped a long finger, one now lightly tanned, on the closed laptop set in the center of the desk. "As it happens, I finished my research a few minutes ago."

She hesitated for two ticks of the old office clock. "Care to share what you discovered?" Although the words were issued in the most casual of tones, her expression had turned watchful, Adam noted, as if she had already guessed more than he'd told her. And it was time to tell her, he knew.

"The plain truth," he said, as gently as he could

manage, "is that I'd rather not share this particular news, but I'm afraid I have no choice." He straightened in his seat and met Jane's gaze head-on. "The reality of the situation is that Glory Ridge doesn't have a hope of competing in its target market, not in this area."

For the blink of an eye, she stilled completely, taking that soft yet frank statement in. "I know it doesn't have much hope of competing the way it is now, but once it's fixed up—"

He stopped her with an upraised palm, deciding it would be kinder not to let her go on. "Even fixed up, the chances of it returning the money invested are slim to none. Everything I've learned about resorts in this area geared to the outdoor crowd indicates that what you could do with the resources you have here is already being done, and by outfits with far newer facilities. You might pull in some business with bargain-basement rates, but not nearly enough to justify the renovation costs."

Somehow, he wasn't surprised when the light of battle sparked in her eyes. "So are you saying I should just give up?"

Not likely, he thought. That would probably earn him a glare sharp enough to pierce skin. "No," he assured her, "I'm not saying that."

"Then what are you saying?" she huffed.

He set his jaw and resisted the temptation to match her terse tone. "If I'd been given a chance to finish before you hit the ceiling, I would have pointed out what I began to suspect at the very start of this job."

"And that would be?"

"That you've got to have an angle to make this thing work."

A quick frown knitted her forehead. "An angle?"

"Yes," he said, and gave the best explanation he could come up with. "You need something the current competition doesn't offer to draw business here. Something different enough to be completely outside the box."

"And what the heck would that be?"

He raked a frustrated hand through his hair. "Damned if I know. Don't think I haven't thought about it, because I have. In fact, I've been racking my brain for days."

His frank admission seemed to take the wind out of her sails, and her frown eased. "I never really expected you to pull off a miracle," she said more quietly, as though recalling his earlier contention that one might be necessary to ensure Glory Ridge's survival. "When I asked for your advice, my plan was to get an expert opinion on the whole thing—and I guess I just got it."

She had, but that didn't stop his insides from twisting at the knowledge that he'd failed to produce a viable strategy to help her. He now had little doubt that saving this place meant as much to her as his son meant to him. Glory Ridge, for all its failings, was beautiful to her, he knew. He'd seen it in her eyes.

"I'm sorry," he said with total truth.

One corner of her mouth quirked upward. "For what it's worth, I think you did your best."

"Not hardly," he countered, feeling the weight of his failure. "At my best, I would have been able to come up with something."

She met that comment with sheer silence. Adam figured he'd probably feel better if she were ranting and raving at him. Then he could indulge in the urge to rant and rave himself. But, just when he would have welcomed her temper, she wasn't going to oblige him, he was all but certain.

Not that she was giving up, even after his far-from-happy news. Somehow, he was all but certain of that, too.

She confirmed it in the next breath. "As Aunt Maude used to say, sometimes you just have to put one foot in front of the other and keep going, like an old-time bride headed down the aisle at a shotgun wedding who's dead sure her daddy will pepper the groom's backside as soon as they're hitched."

Despite everything, a small smile tugged at Adam's lips. "That paints quite a picture. It's definitely a devil of a way to start a honey—"

Suddenly, his voice died in his throat as an idea hit. For days, a workable plan to ensure a healthy future for Glory Ridge had eluded him. Now, images swept through his mind in rapid succession. Brides...grooms...weddings.

And what usually followed.

Summoning the inner instincts he'd honed to a fine edge, he quickly merged them with his past business experience. Then he added everything he'd learned about the resorts in the area to the mix, and after several moments of careful consideration, he came to an unmistakable conclusion.

"That's it!" He slapped a hand on the desk hard enough to rattle its contents. "I've been doing my damnedest to figure out how to make this place turn a consistent profit, and it's been right in front of me all along."

Jane sat forward. "Are you telling me you've had a brainstorm?"

"Yeah, that's as good a description as any."

She moved to the edge of her chair, clearly catching his excitement. "Well, spill it."

He didn't hesitate to comply, although he had to wonder how she would take it. It would be interesting, he decided, to find out. "If the current competition for the usual hiking and fishing crowd prevents successful entry into that market," he said, "the answer is to cater to another sort of guest."

She mulled that over. "The sort of guest who'd want to come here, but not to hike or fish."

"Not primarily, no."

"Hmm. Bird watchers?"

"Not quite." He waited a deliberate beat. "More like lovebirds."

She blinked. *"What?"*

"Lovebirds in the form of newlyweds," he explained.

She gaped at him.

And Adam just kept going, his voice low yet ringing with conviction. "Everything—my brain, my gut and every scrap of business know-how I've developed—is telling me that one sure way to stop this place from sliding even further down the road to ruin is to turn it into a honeymoon resort."

IT TOOK A FEW SECONDS for Jane to even realize that she'd popped out of her chair. "Have you gone clear around the bend?" she bluntly asked the man still seated across from her.

She got an equally blunt reply. "No." Adam

braced his forearms on the desk. "Just hear me out, okay?"

She didn't want to hear him out. "Is this what they pay you the big bucks for? To come up with off-the-wall ideas?"

"I get paid," he informed her, narrowing his gaze, "to help businesses add to their bottom line. And in my estimation, this 'off-the-wall idea', as you put it, will do that for you. Now, do you want to keep an open mind while I tell you how I arrived at that conclusion or not?"

Don't let your temper take over, Jane's more practical side told her. *As crazy as his current plan might sound, this man is still a well-regarded consultant.*

"Okay, I'll listen," she agreed.

"Good," he shot back.

"Keeping an open mind, however, isn't going to be easy," she couldn't resist adding.

"Because you really do think I've gone around the bend," he finished in short order. "I could promise you I haven't. Instead, I'll just say my piece."

She widened her stance and folded her arms. "I'm ready."

He shifted in his chair. "To begin with, nothing in the extensive research I've done indicates that any of the comparable resorts in the area is targeting the newlywed market. That gives Glory Ridge a major advantage because it will be unique. Even if someone else tries to go the same route later, being first in any venture is a big plus."

Jane couldn't help thinking that what he'd said so far made sense, but... "But why would a bunch of newlyweds want to come here?"

"They wouldn't," he told her flatly. "Not as

things stand now. The trick will be to not only renovate the place, but give it a new slant, one that will win some notice.'' Judging by the gleam that sparked in his gaze, Adam was warming to his topic. ''Glory Ridge Resort and Campground is too general a name to suit the purpose. On the other hand, something along the lines of Glory Ridge Honeymoon Haven could be just the ticket.''

Jane had to stare. She also had to wonder how Aunt Maude would react if she were here. ''Glory Ridge *Honeymoon Haven*.''

He didn't so much as blink at her incredulous tone. ''Yes. It's simple and to the point. By and large, that's usually the best way to go,'' he assured her, ''because it tends to stick with the public. Then you build an image from there, as in 'an intimate getaway for two among the tall pines.'''

Jane was fascinated despite herself. ''And that's going to have people primed to come up here?''

''Not people,'' he countered. ''Lovers.''

Lovers. For a hushed moment the word hung in the air between them, filled with the promise of passionate nights. Jane told herself that she had no intention of letting her pulse pick up a beat in response. It did anyway.

When Adam rose and slid a narrow hip on the edge of the desk, putting him that much nearer, she almost took a step back. But she stopped herself. *Always stand your ground, girl,* Maude had told her, *especially when dealing with the male of the species.* As far as Jane was concerned, that was some of the best advice she'd ever received. She wasn't about to forget it.

''The beauty of the whole thing,'' Adam contin-

ued, still clearly enthused, "is that being a small resort will play in Glory Ridge's favor. Even the cabins, which are far from family size, work for this
market—with a few important improvements, of
course."

"Like painting them white with little pink cup-
ids?" Jane asked in a voice ripe with irony. The image she'd offered was the most outrageous thing she
could come up with on short notice. She was back
to staring when he actually seemed to weigh the merits of her suggestion.

"White's not a bad notion," he answered at last.
"It would brighten them up, which would be a plus.
But I was really considering changing out at least
some of the furniture, especially in the bedrooms."
He tapped a finger thoughtfully on the desk. "New
beds are a must, of course, maybe with some of those
five-star mattresses the other resort touted."

His last words became a swift, and not all that
comfortable, reminder of their earlier conversation.
He hadn't bounced on a mattress with anyone lately,
Jane remembered him saying. And she'd admitted as
much herself.

"Come to think of it," he said, still caught up in
his plan, "there'd be no need for a second bedroom
in the cabins that have two. The guest rate for those
could be upped considerably if the spare room were
outfitted with a hot tub."

She hadn't believed her eyes could widen any
more than they had at his first mention of a honeymoon resort. She'd been wrong. "A hot tub!"

"It would probably go over quite well," he told
her. "Not that there aren't other things to consider.
For instance, I can't imagine many newlyweds would

be eager to stay in a cabin called Squirrel Hollow. But with a new name…'' He drifted to a halt, appearing lost in thought.

"Squirrel Hollow's been plenty good enough until now," Jane pointed out.

He snapped his fingers. "But Sweet Seclusion would be better—a lot better for a honeymoon place. Eagle's Nest, being a bit higher than the rest of the cabins, could become, say, Heavenly Hideaway. And Angler's Lair, down by the lake?'' He hesitated, his forehead knitting in concentration. Then his brow cleared. "Ah, I have it. Lovers' Retreat.''

Lovers. Again the word hovered in the air, and this time she wasn't alone in sensing it. At least, Jane suspected as much when the shrewd gleam in Adam's gaze began to cloud with hints of something that had little to do with business. She didn't want to feel the pull of those smoky gray eyes. And felt it anyway.

Suddenly annoyed beyond bearing, chiefly with herself, she took a long step forward and lifted her chin a sharp notch, putting her and Adam nearly nose-to-nose. "If I should decide to go along with this plan—and that's a big *if*—Pitt's Pride stays Pitt's Pride,'' she told him in no uncertain terms.

"I'm not about to argue the point," he replied just as firmly after a second of stark silence.

"Good,'' Jane shot back even as she realized how much of a mistake her last rash step forward had been. It put her near enough to him to take in the scent of plain pine soap with no trace of fancy cologne. The mosquitoes must have won that battle. But he didn't need anything more than soap to smell good. He was close enough for her to figure that out, as well. Too double-darn close.

And still she didn't move.

Neither did Adam. "Getting in a man's face isn't always the smartest thing to do," he told her, his voice turning husky.

She already knew that this time it had been downright foolish. Nevertheless, her pride wouldn't let her back down. "I do as I please."

His gaze bored into hers for taut seconds as the budding tension in the room rose to new heights. "In that case," he said at length, "I'll consider myself free to do likewise." Reaching out, he circled his strong arms around her. In the next breath, his mouth came down on hers.

And then he kissed her, long and hard and deep. Kissed her until she found herself kissing him back as she fisted her hands in his denim shirt. A niggling voice warned that she'd be having second thoughts later about the wisdom of her actions, but she was too caught up in the here and now to pay it much mind. Right this minute, all she wanted to do was relish both the moment and the tangy male taste of the man who continued to kiss the bejeezus out of her.

Eventually, they had to come up for air. Both filled their lungs full, as if they'd surfaced from an ocean dive. But no one moved and their mouths remained inches apart.

"I'm not finished," Adam said at last in a rough whisper that swept a warm breath across her lips.

"Neither," she replied, "am I." And then she reached up, wound her fingers in his silky dark hair, and launched them on another knock-your-socks-off kiss.

Chapter Six

Adam knew he had to call a halt to the whole thing. He couldn't risk the already tenuous grip he had on his control slipping away completely, so he had to stop kissing the woman locked in his arms—and sooner rather than later.

But not yet, the most male parts of him all but growled in his ear. At the moment, he was more than ready to listen to their demands. Once he had wondered how Jane's lips would taste under his. Now he knew. Her small, bare mouth was surprisingly, amazingly, sweet. Sweet enough to be downright addictive.

She'd turned out to be a passionate woman, as well. Perhaps that was even more surprising. Something told him she just might be surprised by that herself. Maybe it was his ego talking, suggesting that he could be the first man to breach her defenses and discover a well-hidden sensuality. Whatever the case, she seemed to be holding nothing back, not now. In fact, she appeared to be as caught up in what was happening as he was.

And he was caught, all right.

Adam couldn't hold back the sudden groan that

rose in his throat. He also couldn't recall a time when he'd been this involved in a kiss. But then, in his current state, his brain had trouble recalling anything. The truth was, thinking at all was getting harder with the way his blood threatened to leave his head and sink past his belt.

Again the two of them came up for air. But this time only instants passed before another kiss was launched. Her hands tightened in his hair. His arms held her securely to him. Both slanted their mouths for a better fit, once again tasting their fill.

Go for it, Adam's libido began to urge. *Go for it all.*

He was so far gone that he was actually considering the merits of acting on that advice. Then he heard a familiar creak as the outside door to the cabin opened. Going for it, even if he won a surprisingly passionate woman's agreement, was no longer an option, he knew. He had to end this, and end it now.

Adam tore his mouth away. "We're about to have company," he said hoarsely, dropping his arms.

Jane's eyes popped open. "Company?" The word was barely out when she pulled her hands from his hair and moved a swift step back.

He cleared his throat. "It's probably Sam."

But that assumption was wrong, as both discovered when a stranger abruptly appeared in the doorway to the office.

"Hello there, folks," the sturdily built, broadshouldered man who appeared to be in his late thirties said in an easy drawl. Sporting a thick thatch of brown hair that was beginning to gray at the temples, he wore a checked shirt, well-used jeans and equally well-used boots. "I'm Curt Bartlett. I called last week about reserving a spot in your campground for my RV.''

Jane took her turn at throat clearing before stepping forward to greet her new guest. ''We weren't expecting you until tomorrow.''

''Made better time than I thought.''

She introduced herself, then aimed a glance back at Adam, one that didn't come close to meeting his eyes. ''And this is Adam Lassiter. He and his son are staying at Glory Ridge. He's also,'' she added, ''been helping me with a, uh, business project.''

The stranger had no trouble meeting Adam's eyes. Or making a swift assessment across the width of the room. Adam caught a glint of what might well be a shrewd intelligence lurking there, before the man's gaze became as casually friendly as his tone. ''Pleased to meet you, Lassiter,'' he offered with a nod.

''Same here,'' Adam replied with a nod in return, although he wasn't sure he meant it. For some reason, the guy put him on edge. Maybe because he suspected Bartlett hadn't failed to observe—despite an obvious bid to pull herself together—that Jane looked like a well-kissed woman.

As for himself... Yeah, he probably presented an image that was a long way from calm, cool and collected.

Adam lifted a hand and did a hasty job of smoothing back his hair. Putting up a calm front when your body was all but shouting in frustration at being denied its way was hard. And his body was; no doubt about it.

Not that he should be complaining. Giving in to the sudden and almost irresistible temptation to kiss

Jane Pitt had hardly been the wisest thing he'd ever done. At least, that was what his brain contended, now that rational thought had resurfaced. He should be grateful, it said, for the interruption. Somehow though, he couldn't quite manage it.

"I'll show you where the hookup for the electricity is," Jane told the new arrival. "Since you might have the only RV parked at the campground for the next few weeks, you've got your choice of which spot to take."

Curt glanced from her to Adam and back again. "I can wait awhile if I've interrupted something."

"You didn't interrupt anything important," Jane said firmly. She met Adam's gaze at last with a rapid look over her shoulder. "Nothing important at all."

So she plans to act as though those kisses didn't matter, Adam reflected. Well, that suited him. He was ready to forget the whole episode—everything but his newly hatched idea. He remained convinced it would work.

"Just remember to give some consideration to what we talked about," he told her.

She hesitated for a moment, then nodded. "All right. I will." And she left with her new guest in tow.

Adam sighed and sank back in his chair. It was time to calm down for real, he told himself. And past time to wipe out the taste of the woman he'd been ready to gobble up in one greedy swallow.

Fat chance, said something that bypassed his brain and came straight from his gut.

Hell. He'd done without an intimate relationship for too long. Adam came to that conclusion as he switched off the desk lamp and propped his booted feet on the desk. Much too long, if a woman who was a far cry from the sleekly sophisticated type he'd been drawn to in the past could stir his juices—the same woman he still had to work with, because he'd made a commitment and he wasn't bailing.

The bottom line was that he had to put what had happened behind him and concentrate on business. The honeymoon business, if Glory Ridge's owner decided to go for it. Would she? Adam asked himself as he stared out a bare window into the dark night. Surely after the bleak news he'd given her earlier, she'd realize that her options were hardly abundant. And if she did, what would she do then?

What she had to do. And without whining about it.

Adam was suddenly certain of that. If no other choice was open to her, she'd take his advice. She might not like it, but the odds were that she'd take it. Because the most important thing to her was saving Glory Ridge.

And the kisses they'd shared? Well, as she'd said, they weren't important at all, not to her.

Nor to him, Adam assured himself. His best bet was to follow her example and forget them...if he could.

SHE COULDN'T FORGET THEM. Not that she hadn't tried. She'd tried like the devil to wipe out the memory of those kisses, Jane thought with a scowl as she left Pitt's Pride the following morning and let the screen door shut behind her.

As though she'd been waiting, Sweet Pea ambled out through a narrow opening dug into the dirt that led to her home beneath the porch floor. A white stripe starting just past her dark eyes and running clear to a bushy tail gleamed against black fur.

"I know I'm late with breakfast," Jane said. She crouched and placed a small plastic bowl filled with high-fiber cereal and a few apple wedges on the bottom porch step. "I had a hard time getting going."

What she'd really had a hard time doing was gearing up to face Adam this morning, Jane admitted to herself. She wasn't admitting that to anyone else, though. Not even to a skunk.

Sweet Pea sniffed the food and soon began to munch on it while Jane sat down on the top porch step. "I guess, since I was late, I can keep you company for a while."

Lame, Jane's conscience told her. As excuses went, that was about as lame as it got. She had plenty to do, and here she was, doing nothing so she wouldn't risk running into *him.*

What in the world had gotten into her? Jane asked herself for the umpteenth time. She had not only let Adam Lassiter kiss her for all he was worth, she'd kissed him back for all *she* was worth.

If she closed her eyes right this minute, she'd have no trouble imagining that his mouth was still locked on hers. That was why she was keeping them firmly open.

"Don't let any pesky male skunks within a mile of you," she advised her companion in a mutter. "You won't get any babies out of the deal, thanks to being fixed, but those pesky males will still complicate your life, trust me."

Sweet Pea raised her head, glanced Jane's way and went back to her breakfast.

"Before you know it," Jane groused, "you'll be

wondering what the heck happened to your peace of mind. And then you'll have to work hard to get it back again.''

Which she would do, Jane vowed. She would keep plugging and return to the woman she'd been—one who wouldn't even have considered tangling tongues with a fancy man.

But first she had to get through this day.

Jane stood, squared her shoulders and started down a winding path through the pines. First thing on her agenda, she decided, was to check the campground and make sure that her new guest had settled in with no problems. Not that she expected any. Curt Bartlett knew what he was doing when it came to spending time in a place long on scenic wonders and short on creature comforts. She'd come to that conclusion after only a brief conversation before she'd left him for the evening. He was no stranger to roughing it, that was plain.

And he didn't bear any resemblance to a person who was out of his element, either. Not like another man she could name.

Jane's gaze landed on that tall, denim-clad man as she came around a bend in the path and approached Squirrel Hollow cabin. Okay, so Adam didn't seem so foreign to this place as he had on first arriving here. With his arms crossed over his chest and one shoulder propped against a narrow porch column, he at least appeared at ease. He didn't look anywhere near as frayed around the edges as she felt, that was for sure.

Jane was so busy resenting that fact it took her a moment to realize that the thoroughly relaxed male who'd kissed her witless the evening before wasn't alone. She felt her eyebrows wing up in surprise. She couldn't imagine what Floyd Crenshaw, Harmony's longtime barber, was doing here. But she supposed she'd find out.

The lanky man with sandy hair liberally threaded with gray greeted her with a smile. Today he'd abandoned his white barber coat for a casual knit shirt and slacks. "Nice to see you," he said to Jane as she stopped beside the porch and viewed both men.

She spared Adam a fleeting glance before fixing her attention on Floyd. "Nice to see you, too. If you've come in your official capacity," she added with deliberate lightness, "I usually cut my own hair."

As he studied her, the older man's gaze took on an amused gleam that said, *it sure wasn't done by a pro.* "Actually, I'm on your doorstep, so to speak, as vice president of the Harmony Business Council. I've been telling Adam, who I hear is passing along some advice business-wise, that the council voted at our meeting last night to give businesses in the area a boost by holding a fair the week after next on the grounds of Courthouse Square."

Jane frowned. "A fair?"

Floyd nodded. "That's a high-toned word for it, I guess. What it means is that we'll set up tables on the lawn, where visitors can stop by and get some info on what Harmony has to offer. A lot of the store owners in town who were at the meeting have already signed up, and other businesses are welcome. With the tourist season in full swing, we should be able to drum up plenty of attention. Thought you might want to join in."

And promote what? Jane thought. A run-down resort her expert consultant had told her was headed straight down the road to ruin? Or would be headed there, unless…

"Can we get back to you on that?" Adam asked, as though he'd sensed the reason for her hesitation.

"Sure thing. You know where to find me," Floyd said. His thin lips curved in a smile as he looked at Adam. "I gave you your first haircut, you might remember. You didn't put up too much of a fuss, as I recall. Still have a fine head of hair, I see. Nice and thick."

It feels as soft as silk, too, when you run your fingers through it. Jane wiped that reflection out in the next breath. Barely restraining herself from fisting her hands at her sides in sheer frustration with her wayward thoughts, she plastered her own version of a smile on her face.

"We'll definitely get back to you," she told Floyd. "Thanks for stopping by."

The barber departed with a jaunty wave, and Jane was left with no choice but to face her consultant. "I suppose we need to talk. About business," she hastened to clarify.

"Just name the time and place," he said, his expression revealing nothing as he stared down at her.

She came to the swift conclusion she'd rather not meet him at the office. The memory of what had happened there was too new. "Down by the lake. After lunch."

"Got it."

The words were scarcely out when Jane switched around and moved away at a brisk clip, telling herself that she was glad she'd faced him and gotten it over with. And she hadn't done anything as mortifying as blushing, thank goodness.

Now she had to decide, and probably sooner rather than later, if she really wanted to follow his advice and turn a resort long known for its simple rustic setting into a haven for newlyweds. *Complete with hot tubs.*

As her feet crunched on bare gravel, she had to wonder one more time what Aunt Maude would think about the whole thing.

"OKAY, SUPPOSING I did decide to turn this place into a honeymoon resort. What would be the next step?"

The woman seated beside him on the old wooden dock still wasn't jumping at the idea, Adam noted, even though she realized that her choices were severely limited. Jane had accepted that much, he was certain. Otherwise, they probably wouldn't be discussing his plan at all.

"Next," he said, "you'd hire someone to start fixing up the place, keeping in mind the sort of improvements I suggested. Meanwhile, I could get started on putting some initial advertising material together. You've got a golden opportunity to capitalize on this promotional fair the business council is running. It'd be a shame not to take advantage of it."

"Yeah, I've been thinking the same thing," she confessed, shifting in her seat.

Adam refrained from following her example. He didn't need a stray splinter piercing his backside. "I've done a good deal of thinking myself," he told her. Not about how she'd felt in his arms. No, he was avoiding that particular memory.

"A major advantage in catering to newlyweds," he went on, "is that there's a continual supply of them year-round. And then there's always the possibility that they'll want to celebrate anniversaries here, too. It certainly wouldn't hurt to send cards out every year, wishing them a happy anniversary and reminding them of their stay at Glory Ridge."

"Hmm." Jane stared straight ahead, looking across the sun-splashed lake rather than at her companion.

But Adam was well aware that he was making progress. "That's the key to a successful operation— not only steady business but repeat business."

"So we rename the resort," she said after a moment.

"Yes."

"And the cabins."

"All except Pitt's Pride," he assured her. The last thing he wanted was a repeat of yesterday's confrontation. Who knows what would happen if she got in his face again and lifted that stubborn little chin. He'd rather not test it. Not today.

Jane kept staring straight ahead. To Adam's mind, it was time to put forth the one argument that had a real hope of swaying her. "With these changes, the resort stands a good chance of not only being around years from now, but thriving. Without them…" He deliberately left that last statement hanging and waited for a response. He'd learned the value of patience when dealing with a client.

Silent minutes passed before she slowly turned her

head and stared him straight in the eye. "Okay. I'll do it."

"Good." He kept his voice casual, even though a sense of victory rose inside him. Someday, he told himself, when she was making a regular profit, she'd be damn thankful that she'd taken his advice. Many others he'd helped in the past had come to feel that way. She would, too.

Of course, he wouldn't be here to enjoy watching Jane admit that he'd been right. By then, the summer would be over and he'd be gone. He'd just have to enjoy his victory from a distance and look back on his time in the great outdoors as a learning experience.

He wouldn't regret coming to Glory Ridge, he knew. But he'd be glad to get back on more familiar ground. There was no denying he missed many of the things he'd left behind. Then, too, he couldn't help feeling that this place would someday seem more like something conjured by his imagination than stark reality, as though he'd never really been a part of it.

He didn't belong here, Adam thought. It was as simple as that.

Jane regained his attention with a soft yet heartfelt sigh, as if resigning herself to the inevitable. "How soon do you think this whole thing can be up and running?"

"Since you already have enough savings to proceed, I'd aim for early to mid fall. As I remember from my years in Harmony, this area gets a good many visitors when the trees start to turn. It would be an additional drawing point, and that can't hurt. Right now, the most important thing is to get the word out, and one way to start is to make an impact at the upcoming business fair. I can help with that.''

She lifted a brow. ''I guess we'll have to pass out some fancy brochures.''

''No doubt about it,'' he informed her. ''You have to show them what you've got and tout its virtues. I can take some photographs of Quail Lake and the woods around it, which are your biggest assets at the moment. Getting one cabin done, at least on the outside, would be a plus, too. Considering what could be used to its best advantage in a photo, I vote for the one closest to the lake.''

She glanced at the cabin in question, Angler's Lair. ''Getting it in shape probably won't take too long.''

''Don't forget to tack a new name on the door,'' he reminded her. He'd proposed Lovers' Retreat, he remembered.

As though she recalled it, as well—both his proposed name and what had followed—Jane cleared her throat. ''Right. You can snap pictures of whatever you want,'' she said, rushing on, ''as long as I don't have to be in any of them.''

''You don't,'' he assured her, ''but—'' He broke off, wondering how best to phrase what he had to say next.

''But what?'' she asked after a beat.

He decided to just wade in. ''With the upcoming fair, you might consider making some changes in your wardrobe.''

Her sudden frown came as no surprise. ''Are you saying I have to get dressed up for this thing?''

He met her gaze and held it. ''You'll be meeting

potential customers, and you'll have to impress them.''

Her frown deepened. ''With the resort, sure.''

''That's a given—but its owner is part of the package,'' he pointed out with total honesty.

For a moment, she looked stunned, as though she'd never considered that aspect of promotion. Her mouth opened and closed without so much as a sound. In the end, she wound up staring at him in utter silence, her frown still firmly in place.

Well, at least you didn't tick her off enough to have her trying to shove you off the dock, Lassiter. Deciding to let the subject drop for now, he said, ''Just think about it, okay?''

''Hey, Dad,'' Sam called from where he'd been casting a line into the water farther along the winding shore. ''My hook's stuck in the weeds.''

Adam might not have landed a fish yet, but he'd become an expert at untangling a line. Allowing himself at least some small satisfaction at that accomplishment, he got to his feet. ''Be right there,'' he called back.

Jane watched him walk away. Despite the fact that he'd just stunned her into silence, she didn't miss how snug denim hugged his narrow hips. Or how he seemed to move with a natural male grace. She should be grateful that he was gone, she thought. Too bad some wayward parts of her hadn't received the message.

Something told her she'd be in trouble, big trouble, if she couldn't go back to viewing him as merely her consultant. Oh, yes. She would be.

Jane let out a lengthy breath, deciding that maybe what she needed was to see him in a pricey suit, like the one he wore when he'd first arrived on her door-step. Dressed to the nines, he'd been. If she could just keep that picture firmly in mind, things might be okay. If she couldn't, it wouldn't be easy, not hardly, to work with him.

But she had to do it, regardless. She knew that much full well. She still needed his business savvy, maybe now more than ever. Good Lord, she had no idea how to tackle something as foreign to her as a honeymoon spot.

"You'll learn, though," she muttered, "because you have to."

She would have to get used to the sight of new-lyweds batting their eyes at each other all over the place, maybe even cooing like turtledoves to boot. By the lake, on the paths, in the woods.

One corner of Jane's mouth quirked upward. If they did more than cooing and tried to take things too far in the woods, they just might find out that bare backsides could be a liability there.

Many of them would probably show up to be cud-dled by Mother Nature while they cuddled each other, but nature wasn't always so amenable. In fact, sometimes the old gal could be downright cranky, and during those times it didn't do to cross her. That was a lesson some people had to learn the hard way.

Then again, she was used to looking out for green-horns on occasion, Jane reminded herself. This would just be a new breed. Still, she supposed she'd have to dredge up more tact than she'd had to in the past when dealing with the outdoor crowd. She'd have to handle her guests with kid gloves, smile a lot for no reason and wish them a cheery hello every day—if not several times a day—even if what she really longed to do was make herself scarce so she wouldn't have to watch newlyweds being…newlyweds.

In short, she as well as the resort, would have to change.

Which is basically what her hotshot consultant had just told her, she realized. It wasn't something she'd bargained on, that was for sure, yet there was no point in hiding her head in the sand. She couldn't greet guests, not *these* guests, wearing clothes a lot of people would consider candidates for the rag pile.

And that was just for starters. There was her hair, too, which she never paid much attention to until some had to be hacked off. And her face, which she'd never fussed over. She'd watched other girls, including her sister, primp before a mirror. She, however, had never seen the point, not for herself.

Jane leaned forward and viewed her image in the rippling blue water. She saw what she'd been seeing for too many years to count—and it just didn't measure up.

The bald truth was, at the moment she doubted she stood a chance of winning a scrap of new business. Couples seeking an out-of-the-way spot, one in competition with ritzy hotels, swanky cruises and who knows what else for honeymoon dollars, would take one look at her and decide to spend their money elsewhere. All at once she was as sure of that as she was of her own name.

Jane closed her eyes. Good grief, she needed help.

Chapter Seven

"You've come to the right place," Ellen said confidently as she studied her sister. "And it's about time," she added dryly.

Jane acknowledged that she wouldn't be visiting Cuts 'N Curls at all if she'd had a choice. The sunny morning was a lot more suited for overseeing the construction crew now beginning to tackle the job of fixing up the cabins. Not that they needed any supervision. She'd checked out the local firm before signing the contract. It had a reputation for doing excellent work in a reasonable amount of time—at a reasonable price. Which was good enough for her.

Still, she'd rather be watching the burly foreman and his two-man crew patch up the roof of the cabin by Quail Lake. Heck, she'd rather be doing almost anything besides trying her best not to squirm under her sister's can't-wait-to-get-my-hands-on-you gaze.

Jane leaned a hip against the side of the work station. "I just need a little sprucing up for this business fair," she told Ellen, repeating the explanation she'd given on the phone, when she'd also passed along the news that Glory Ridge was soon to be a "honeymoon haven."

Ellen crossed her arms over her bright peach smock. The gleam in her eyes didn't dim a watt. "A little won't do it."

Jane swallowed. "Sure it will."

Ellen aimed a glance at her fellow hairdresser, Dot Donahue. "What do you think?"

Dot studied Jane every bit as thoroughly as Ellen had and shook her head, sending a mass of dyed-red ringlets dancing in the air. She was in her forties and had a figure with plenty of lush curves. "Major work" was Dot's frank judgment.

Major. The word threatened to have sweat breaking out on Jane's brow. In sheer self-defense, she appealed to Leslie Hanson, a nurse at the medical center and Dot's current customer. "It can't be as bad as that."

Leslie followed Dot's example and shook a head topped by short, silver waves. "I'm afraid it is," she told Jane in the nicest way possible.

"That's three against one," Ellen declared, looking her sister straight in the eye. "Good thing I have the whole morning free. We'll need time—a lot of time."

A lot of time. Jane stood her ground when her feet wanted to run. "A haircut and a quick makeup lesson can't take that long."

Ellen released a gusty sigh. "Your hair needs not only a good cut but conditioning."

"Heavy duty," Dot added.

"And maybe a highlighter," Ellen went on. "I use one to add shine to my hair." As though attesting to that, her blond curls glistened under the overhead light.

Well, the full treatment was fine for her sister, Jane

thought, but her own goal was the least muss and fuss possible. "Oh, that can't all be necess—" she started to say.

"It's necessary," Ellen countered firmly. "And before we can even get to a makeup lesson, you need to have a facial and tweeze those brows."

Jane nearly winced. "My eyebrows are fine without being tortured by a pair of blasted tweezers."

"Don't be a chicken." Ellen headed for the back of the shop. "Come on, let's get you shampooed."

Jane followed, refusing to drag her steps. She had asked for Ellen's help, she reminded herself. And she kept reminding herself as her newly shampooed hair was snipped.

Ellen leaned in with the scissors and murmured in her sister's ear. "Besides the upcoming fair, this wouldn't have anything to do with Adam Lassiter, would it?"

"Not a bit," Jane muttered. And it didn't, she assured herself. She was doing this for Glory Ridge. Period.

Ellen met Jane's gaze in the mirror. "Then I take it he's still not making your heart flutter?"

"I won't even dignify that with a reply." Because if she did, she'd have to lie. She certainly didn't plan on mentioning those kisses and how they'd made her heart flutter plenty.

"Hmm." Ellen's expression turned thoughtful. "He may do it yet. The man seems resourceful."

This time Jane kept her mouth shut, remembering that her sister had had only praise for Adam's plan to save the resort.

"Conditioner's next." Ellen got back to business and began to work in a thick cream.

Jane sniffed. "Smells like apples."

"It has a fruit base and lots of good stuff." Ellen wrapped Jane's hair in a warm towel and leaned the chair back as far as it would go. "Just relax. We have to leave that to work for a while. I'll put the facial mask on, then I'm going to run out and buy some makeup. My skin tones are warmer than yours, so mine won't suit you."

Jane fumbled under the cape tied at her neck and shoved a hand into her jeans pocket. "I'll give you some money."

"Consider it a present," Ellen said.

"No way."

"Yes."

"Why?"

"Because I want to." Ellen grinned. "Actually, I'm having so much fun, making you pay would be a crime."

That Jane could believe, so she stopped arguing. She didn't even complain—not too much, at any rate—when Ellen smoothed some gunk on her face. Nor did she protest when her sister departed with the news that Dot would remove the mask, rinse Jane's hair and deal with the highlighter.

Instead, she just closed her eyes and endured, even restraining a groan when Dot suggested a manicure. "Oh, I don't really think that's necess—"

"It is." Dot cut her off even more bluntly than Ellen had earlier.

"I think you should," another voice said.

Jane opened an eye. "Aren't you finished?" she asked Dot's last customer.

Leslie smiled down at her. "I can't leave now and miss the transformation."

"Humph." Jane snapped her eye shut and did her best to concentrate on something else. She soon found she was a lot more comfortable thinking about Glory Ridge's transformation than her own. That, at least, was going well.

Besides the work being started on the cabins, Sam had told her before she'd left for town that he and his father planned to take pictures around the resort that morning. The best of their photos would go in the new brochure, which would be mailed to responders to an ad in a popular bridal magazine as well as handed out at the fair.

Floyd had been pleased to hear that the resort would participate in the event when she'd dropped by his barbershop to tell him the news. "Maude Pitt would be proud of you," he'd told Jane on learning that Glory Ridge would target a brand-new sort of customer.

Jane had blinked at that. "You don't think she'd be…" *Appalled* was the first word that came to mind, but she couldn't quite get it out. "Upset" was what she settled on.

Floyd's thin lips had quirked at the corners. "She might be surprised. I wouldn't even say no to flabbergasted. But she never strayed from her goal of keeping the place going, no matter what. Actually, I think she'd give you a big pat on the back," he'd summed up with a fatherly wink.

And Jane had felt better for hearing that, she couldn't deny. She still might not be wild about having a bunch of newlyweds mooning at each other all over the place, but if Maude could understand that she'd done what she'd had to do—

"Time for the next step," Ellen said, interrupting

Jane's thoughts. She hadn't realized that her sister had returned. Truth was, she'd hardly been aware Dot had removed the mask and rinsed her hair. Then, she'd done her best to tune out her surroundings. Now she was back in the swivel chair and the highlighter had been applied, or so she assumed. She couldn't tell with another towel wound around her head.

Then she saw the shiny silver tweezers in her sister's slender hand. "I *really* don't feel it's necess—"

"It is," a trio of voices said in unison. Ellen looked determined, Dot confident and Leslie amused.

Jane sighed. "Okay, okay." She just had to hope it wouldn't hurt too much.

IT HURT, but she got through the tweezing—and the makeup lesson that followed, although she smeared the powder blusher and almost poked her eye out with the mascara wand before getting the hang of the thing. She also dropped the tube of shell-pink lipstick that matched the blusher after noticing that somewhere along the way her nails had been painted nearly the same shade of pink.

Pink. Jane wanted to moan. It was such a "girly" color.

She settled for retreating behind closed eyes yet again as Ellen started to blow-dry her hair after a last rinse. Finally snapping off the dryer, Ellen asked, "Am I good or am I good?"

"Damn good" was Dot's judgment.

"It's amazing," Leslie added with a soft sigh.

Jane opened her eyes and found that the chair was turned away from the mirror. "Do I get to see?"

"You bet," Ellen said as she removed Jane's cotton cape. Then she whipped the chair around with a practiced spin and Jane got her first look at the final results of her sister's handiwork.

She looked…different, she decided. Not too different, though. She was still the person she'd seen in her mirror every day for too many years to count. Maybe not quite as plain, she had to admit. Her short hair was neater and shinier. Her face had more color. But no real beauty stared back at her, not by a long shot.

Then again, she'd never expected one. She'd just wanted to be presentable enough to pass muster, and she guessed she was.

"Thanks," she told Ellen.

"You're welcome." Ellen smiled a wide smile. "I'd be tempted to take a bow, but this transformation isn't over yet."

No, Jane thought. It *had* to be over. There was only so much she could endure, even for Glory Ridge.

Before she could say as much, Ellen departed for the front of the shop, then quickly returned with a large shopping bag from one of Harmony's downtown boutiques. She reached into the bag, pulled out a small, brightly wrapped box and handed it to Jane. "Save this to open later when you get home. It's an early birthday present."

Jane's newly tweezed brows drew together. "My birthday's not until October."

Ellen's smile turned sly. "You may find that you need what's in there before then."

Suspicion narrowed Jane's eyes. They widened in the next breath as Ellen pulled a dress out of the bag—a silky white summer dress strewn with tiny yellow tulips.

"I can't wear that!"

"And why not?" Dot wanted to know.

"It's too much, too...female."

"I think it's darling," Leslie said.

"And you *are* a female," Ellen pointed out even as she ventured into the bag one more time and retrieved a pair of white sandals. "These go with the dress. And you're going to hurt my feelings if you don't take all of this," she warned before Jane could get another word out.

Nothing could have coaxed Jane into submission more. Ever since the youngest Pitt child had been born looking like the most precious, happiest baby ever, Jane had done her best never to hurt her sister. But that didn't stop her from gritting her teeth now and then.

"Okay," she said at last, "I'll take everything."

Ellen crossed her arms under her breasts. "And you'll try on the dress and sandals so we can get the full effect?"

"Uh-huh."

Leslie clapped her hands.

Dot gave Jane's booted feet a long look. "Wouldn't be a bad idea to have a pedicure, since your toes will show in those sandals."

Good grief. Jane grabbed the dress and shoes and beat a swift retreat to the rest room at the back of the shop. Nobody, but nobody, she vowed, was messing with her toes!

ADAM'S FEET, now that his boots were broken in, were as comfortable as the rest of him. He was in his element, he thought with satisfaction as he took yet another shot of Quail Lake. Getting the right angle and setting the correct tone, to show the resort to its best advantage, came easily to him.

This, he knew how to do.

"Good thing I brought my camera, huh?" Sam asked from his father's side.

Adam lined up a wide view of deep blue water backed by tall pines and pushed the shutter. "A very good thing," he agreed. "I think we have enough shots of the lake. As soon as the outside of the first cabin is finished, we'll get a picture of that, too." In the distance he could see the men Jane had hired. They were propping a tall ladder against a log wall.

Sam hitched his new backpack higher on his thin shoulders. "Now we snap some pictures of the woods?"

"Mmm-hmm." Adam considered his plan to combine that project with their first hike together a good one, if he did say so himself. The weight of his own backpack nestled between his shoulder blades felt strange, but he supposed he'd get used to it. Turning, he studied the thick blanket of trees behind them and spied what looked like a narrow trail. "Let's try over there." He started forward, leading the way.

The weather had certainly fallen in with his plans. A light, warm breeze drifted down from the mountains—and there wasn't a cloud in the sky, Adam noted with a fleeting glance above him. Not that he could see much of the sky with the way the trees were closing in. "Hopefully, we'll find a small clearing,'' he said, ''preferably a bit higher up, where we can set up some good shots.''

Hitting upon the sort of spot he had in mind took them a while. The woods closed in even tighter as they moved steadily inland. But eventually a break in the trees appeared. A group of rocks big enough to be called boulders soon came into view.

Sam looked around him. ''How'd these rocks get here?''

Adam mulled that over for a moment. ''Maybe they were tossed here by a blast from an ancient volcano.'' It was the most likely theory he could come up with.

''A volcano. Wow.''

Adam's mouth curved at the wonder in Sam's voice. His son just might be discovering that the distant past could be as fascinating as the far-off future. Not that Sam had given up wearing his space-themed T-shirts or reading science fiction. But he'd developed an interest in the world around him, not just worlds found only in the imagination. And that interest clearly extended to a spot Sam would never have chosen to visit—not if he'd had a choice.

The irony of it, Adam thought, was that these days Sam seemed to feel far more at home at Glory Ridge than his father did.

''The top of that biggest rock might be a good spot to take some pictures. Think you can climb up there without hurting yourself?'' Adam asked. He figured he owed Sam a chance to practice his photography skills, but safety came first.

Sam nodded. "I can do it."

"Sure?"

"I'm double-darn sure."

Adam didn't miss the fact that Sam's confident statement could have come from Glory Ridge's owner. He wasn't surprised. Sam not only liked Jane's cooking, he appeared a long way from opposed to spending time with her. The boy dreamer who could still lose himself in the stars, and the no-nonsense woman who was rooted to the ground. An unlikely pair, some would say, but they appeared to get along well together.

True to his word, Sam made the climb with no trouble. Adam watched him until the boy gained his footing, then he handed him the camera.

When Sam had snapped a few pictures, Adam took the camera back and tried a few shots of his own from ground level, making a circle around the clearing. He included one of Sam perched on the boulder for his personal collection. He'd find a frame and add it to those he kept on his bedroom dresser back home. After Sam returned to Boston, it would serve as a reminder of the time they'd shared here.

Adam bit back a sigh. He didn't want to think about his son leaving. He'd have to eventually, of course. But not yet.

"How about a candy bar to keep our strength up?" he asked.

Sam acted with predictable enthusiasm for anything in the chocolate family. "Okay!"

Adam held his arms out. "Jump down. I'll catch you."

Sam jumped and landed safely. But he didn't linger in Adam's arms. Instead, he moved a quick step back.

The swift retreat had Adam recognizing that although they'd gradually grown closer, they hadn't regained all the ground that had somehow been lost over the years. Would they? He still had to hope that would happen.

They ate the candy bars Sam pulled from his backpack and followed them up with the bottled water his father carried. "Guess it's time to head back," Adam said at last.

Sam looked up at him. "Which way?"

He aimed a probing glance around the area, searching for the narrow path that had brought them to the clearing. Trouble was, he found two heading off in almost the same direction. Almost, but not quite.

"This way," he said, choosing the path on the right.

Which turned out to be wrong.

It was the only conclusion Adam could come to after they'd walked for the better part of an hour and hadn't come upon the lake. Even worse, when he stopped and looked back, he could hardly make out any sign of a path at all. Retracing their steps and getting back to the clearing wouldn't be easy, he realized.

Okay, where in blazes do you go from here, Lassiter? he asked himself.

Quiet moments passed before Sam followed up

Adam's silent question with a question of his own. "Dad, are we lost?"

Adam's first impulse was to reassure Sam that he had everything under control. Then the memory of something Jane had once said flooded back.

When a man with a growing son is successful at most everything he does, it might not be a bad notion to let a less-confident side of himself show now and then.

This seemed like the ideal time to put that theory into practice. Adam couldn't deny he felt less than confident at the moment. Placing a hand on Sam's shoulder, he opted for the blunt truth. "Yeah, we're lost."

Sam frowned at that news. "Does that mean we might hafta stay out here all night?"

God, Adam had to hope not. As far as he was concerned, sleeping on the lumpy mattress in his current bedroom was bad enough. "I don't think it'll come to that."

"But—" Sam started to say. Then something at one side of the path caught his notice. "Is that Sweet Pea?"

Adam followed his son's gaze and found a skunk standing several feet away, calmly regarding them. "If it's not, we may be in trouble."

Sam swallowed loud enough to be heard.

"But if it is," Adam added, keeping his voice even, "maybe we can trail her back to the resort."

"That would be good," Sam allowed in a whisper.

Damn right. Adam stood stock-still as the skunk approached. He didn't have a clue if it was even male or female, but it was about the same size as Jane's skunk. Only when the animal sniffed Sam's tennis shoes and stared up at the boy did Adam relax.

"It's gotta be Sweet Pea," Sam said.

"I'd say so," Adam agreed, vowing then and there to talk Jane into buying this animal a collar, maybe a rhinestone-studded version guests could see at ten yards. Otherwise, she'd be risking a bunch of newlyweds taking one look and heading for the hills, which would hardly be good for business.

Adam watched as Sweet Pea began to amble back up the path he and Sam had just negotiated. "Come on. Let's follow and see where it gets us."

This time he let Sam take the lead and kept the skunk in sight over the boy's head. "By the way," he said as they threaded their way through the trees, "if we do wind up back at the resort, there's no need to mention that we were lost."

Sam aimed a glance back over his shoulder. "You mean to Jane?"

"Uh-huh. The thing is..." Adam paused, wondering how to word it.

"Guys don't tell about getting lost?" Sam ventured.

"They don't always tell the female half of the population," Adam clarified. "That keeps them from getting too smug," he added under his breath.

This time a crafty grin slanted Sam's mouth when he looked back at his father, as though they were co-conspirators. "Okay, I won't tell."

"Good." Adam flashed a brief grin in return. With any luck at all, he thought, they'd be able to keep that secret to themselves. "Come on, Sweet Pea," he muttered as they continued moving, "be a pal and get us back."

SHE GOT THEM BACK. Their last winding stretch through the trees opened to clear land near the parking lot next to the resort office. A few yards away stood the late-model, dark-green RV belonging to Glory Ridge's latest guest, the only occupant of a small campground that might once have been filled to capacity.

It was a little past one, Adam noted with a glance at his watch. And Jane's truck was nowhere in sight, which meant she hadn't yet returned from her trip to town. She hadn't mentioned why she was going, but grocery shopping seemed the most likely bet to him. Could be the supply of macaroni and cheese—or maybe hot dogs—was running low.

"Good job!" Sam called after Sweet Pea as she continued down the gravel path leading to the cabins. "She doesn't walk too quick, but she knows where she's going," he added with a laugh.

Even Adam had to smile as he watched the skunk depart, and that smile was still in place when the rattle of an ancient engine split the quiet. Seconds later Jane's dusty red pickup roared around a bend in the road. The brakes squealed a protest as she pulled into the lot.

He and Sam waited for her to get out. And waited some more.

Adam's smile widened at the thought that her

nerves might need a minute to recover from that breakneck trip up the mountain.

Then the pickup door opened and Jane hopped out, and his smile disappeared, a victim of sheer shock.

Good Lord was all he could think. His brain knew he wasn't looking at a stranger, but his eyes disagreed! Jane's short, neatly cut hair sparkled in the sunshine, as though threaded with dark gold. Her pink cheeks and lips showed deft enhancement to the blush Mother Nature had supplied. And her floral-print dress, with its fitted bodice and full skirt, displayed a slender figure to advantage—including a pair of shapely, ivory legs and small, well-formed feet all but left bare by thin-strapped sandals.

Adam took a hesitant step forward with Sam at his side. He didn't have to see the surprise on his son's face. He could hear it in Sam's voice when the boy was the first to comment on Jane's appearance.

"Gee, you look like a, uh, girl."

No, much more like a woman, Adam thought, still trying to get his vocal cords working. *All woman.*

"Thanks—I think," Jane told Sam dryly, but the statement was too soft for sarcasm. Then she glanced up at Adam. His gaze met hazel eyes that seemed bigger framed by lashes that looked thicker and darker. "I don't see any reason to stare," she told him, her voice holding a more characteristic bite. "Didn't you say I needed to make some changes?"

"Yes, but I didn't expect..." He cleared his throat. "It may take me a while to get used to the new picture," he confessed. "It's...impressive." He sure as hell was impressed.

"Have to say I agree." Curt Barlett's deep voice rang with good cheer as he approached the group, his large hands crammed into his jean pockets. His eyes made a swift yet thorough study of Glory Ridge's owner and soon lit with an appreciative gleam as he came to a halt.

"You sure do make quite a sight," he told Jane in his easy drawl.

Adam's hands fisted at his sides before he even realized it. He had no logical reason to resent Bartlett's remark. Or that gleam. But there was no denying that he resented both.

Rather than preening under the other man's praise, Jane shrugged off the comment. "I just made a few personal changes to go along with some I plan to make at the resort."

For a moment Curt appeared taken aback by that news. "Changes?"

"Don't worry, they won't affect your stay here," she assured him. She faced Adam. "Did you have any trouble getting the photos you wanted?"

He and Sam exchanged a glance before Adam answered in an offhand tone, "No trouble." *If you don't count needing a skunk to lead us out of the woods.* "We'll have plenty of pictures to choose from, and I think potential customers will like what they see—the perfect spot for a quiet, out-of-the-way honeymoon."

"Honeymoon." Curt's eyes no longer held that gleam. Instead, he looked puzzled.

"I'm getting hungry," Sam murmured to his father as Jane began a more detailed explanation of her plans for the resort. "Can we make a sandwich?"

Adam nodded, then waited for a break in the conversation and told Jane he'd see her later. Trouble was, he couldn't stop seeing her—the *new* her—in his mind as he and Sam headed for their cabin.

Yes, he'd told her that a few changes were in order. The honest truth was, he'd have failed to give her the full benefit of his expertise if he hadn't suggested that she consider some additions to her wardrobe to accompany the resort's revised image.

But she'd gone beyond what he'd had in mind. A long way beyond.

Which was going to make forgetting those kisses ever harder.

Adam frowned. Later that evening, he promised himself, he'd come up with a mental list of all the reasons he should forget each and every minute of that passionate meeting of mouths—and then he'd pound that list into his brain.

But your body, something told him, *is what really needs to be convinced.*

LATER THAT EVENING, her face scrubbed and a large navy T-shirt filling in as nightwear, Jane sat tailor-fashion on her bed. The brightly wrapped box Ellen had given her rested on the worn ivory bedspread. She still hadn't opened the present, half-afraid what she'd find. Goodness knows, she'd had enough to deal with today—including her return to Glory Ridge, which hadn't ended up as expected.

Her idea, formed the minute she'd left Cuts 'N

Curls, was to make it to her cabin and change back into her old clothes before anyone got a glimpse of her. Sure, a lot of people would get more than a glimpse at the upcoming fair. She'd be wearing her new dress to the event—Ellen had pried that promise out of her before Jane had made her getaway. But she hadn't planned on giving anybody at Glory Ridge a sneak preview.

Jane grimaced, recalling how, just to get out of the truck, she'd had to remind herself that she'd never been a coward. And then she'd had to force herself to keep from squirming when all eyes had turned wide at the sight of her. Adam's, she remembered, had been the most startled of the bunch.

Not that she could figure out why he'd looked like somebody had hit him over the head with a two-by-four. She hadn't changed that much.

"Men," she muttered with feeling. "Guess I'll never understand them. Then again, Aunt Maude would probably tell me not to waste time trying."

Jane decided to take that advice and picked up Ellen's present. Might as well get it over with, she decided. She removed the coral ribbon and ginger-print paper, then opened the box, to find a much smaller box resting inside.

"'Passion's Promise,'" she said, reading the gleaming gold label. The name of the perfume, not to mention the tiny winged hearts flapping around it, had her rolling her eyes. She didn't open the box, just sniffed the clear cellophane wrapper, which was all it took to get a potent whiff.

"Whew," she murmured, "this stuff is strong

enough to drown out fish bait. The mosquitoes around here would go crazy.''

She set the perfume on the bed, parted the ivory tissue paper enfolding the rest of the present and pulled out something that had her staring. The simple, thigh-length white nightgown sported a narrow ruffle around the hem and another bordering the high scooped neckline. Jane might have considered it suitable for a schoolgirl…if not for the gauzy fabric that wouldn't hide a freckle.

Did Ellen think she'd ever actually wear this? *This?* Shaking her head, Jane got up, folded the nightgown and put it in the bottom drawer of a small pine dresser far older than she was. She tossed the perfume in after it, sure she'd never wear that, either, and closed the drawer.

Her birthday present, she reflected with a rueful twist of her lips as she headed back to the bed. ''I could have used a new tackle box—or a dozen other things. But no, Ellen has to go off the deep end just because I ask for a little sprucing up.''

Jane bent to pick up the empty box. Only then did she realize there was still something in the bottom, covered by yet another layer of tissue. She investigated and found herself looking down at a stack of small, foil-wrapped packets.

She closed her eyes as recognition hit. Then she snapped them open again, took the box and dumped its contents into an old stoneware honey jar kept on the dresser and converted to a catch-all for pins. The condoms had barely landed in the jar before she jammed the top back on.

Ellen had gone too far, she thought. And she was telling Ellen so in no uncertain terms the next time she saw her, even if her words did land on deaf ears.

Which they probably would, Jane decided, all at once sure why her sister had gone to such lengths to put that gift together. The present had nothing to do with her birthday.

And everything to do with Adam Lassiter.

Ellen figured, despite firm assurances to the contrary, that Jane wouldn't be able to keep her head screwed on straight where a particular fancy man was concerned. Heck, if Ellen ever found out they'd already locked lips, she'd probably pat herself on the back for her foresight in choice of presents.

But Ellen was wrong. She had to be wrong.

Jane nodded briskly and dismissed her sister's perceptiveness with the wave of a hand. Then she noted that hand held five glossy nails painted a creamy and very ''girly'' pink. She returned to the rustic pine bed and sank onto it, thinking that her sister had supplied a bag containing enough makeup, hair products and other ''necessities,'' as Ellen had put it, to last Jane for months. But she'd left something out, either by accident—or more likely on purpose.

Jane sighed, certain there wasn't an ounce of nail-polish remover within miles of Glory Ridge.

Chapter Eight

The fair was well on its way to being a success. Adam decided as much halfway through the crowded event. A haphazard arrangement of long tables covered with crisp white cloths decorated the lush lawn at Courthouse Square. Each held a generous supply of promotional material and giveaway items touting a variety of businesses in the area. Colorful balloons tacked to table corners added a celebratory note to the proceedings, and visitors eager to investigate what participating businesses had to offer were in good supply.

Harmony's Business Council, its own small table located in the center of the square under a tall statue dedicated to the city's founding fathers, had done one hell of a job, Adam thought. He didn't hesitate to say as much when Tom Kennedy strolled by and asked how the event was going.

"Glory Ridge's new brochures seem to be finding favor," he told the police chief. "If you're ever in the market for a honeymoon spot, you're about to get one alternative close by."

The longtime bachelor's chuckle rumbled out of him. "Don't see that happening, but I'll keep it in mind.'' He picked up a brochure and inspected it, opening the three-fold pamphlet to its full length.

Adam couldn't help but feel a sense of accomplishment, knowing what stared back at Tom in vivid color. The best of the pictures he and Sam had taken were now incorporated into the promotional copy Adam had written. He was particularly proud of the shot of the newly painted cabin, its sparkling white exterior standing out against the deep blue lake. The front door sported a heart-shaped sign trimmed in red that declared its name to be Lovers' Retreat. Glory Ridge's owner had rolled her eyes when he'd offered his suggestion for the sign's design, but she'd gone along with it in the end.

And he'd been vindicated, Adam reflected with satisfaction. More than one prospective customer had oohed and aahed over both the cabin and its impressive backdrop. Once he got the pictures up on the Web site he was creating, he hoped to multiply that reaction a thousandfold.

''Excellent job all around'' was Tom's judgment as he refolded the brochure. ''Looks like Glory Ridge is in for some major changes.'' He glanced at the person seated next to Adam behind the long table. ''Seems the resort isn't the only thing that's changed, either,'' he added quietly.

Adam didn't have to follow Tom's gaze to take his meaning. Clearly, he was referring to Jane, who was talking to two middle-aged women. Both had newly engaged daughters, which made them prime marketing targets.

Tom was far from the first person with those sentiments. Others had expressed them mainly by look rather than word. The police chief's current assessment of the new Jane, however, held no more than friendly interest—not always the case with other men that day.

Adam's good mood dimmed as he recalled how some of the men in the milling crowd—many of them a lot younger than the chief—had given Jane a long once-over. Avid, not just friendly interest, would best describe the look in their eyes. He'd been tempted—sorely tempted, truth be told—to glare at them.

"Where's Sam?" Tom asked, again looking at Adam.

"He and Jane's nephew are spending the day together. From what I'm told, they plan to start building a tree house out at the Malloy ranch."

"Travis is a good kid," Tom said. "And Mitch Malloy can be trusted to see that the boys don't tackle anything they can't handle."

Adam had already come to that conclusion. Which was why he'd agreed to Sam's spending not only the day but the night at the Malloy's.

Tom thumbed back his wide-brimmed tan hat, raised his gaze and aimed it to the east, where tall white clouds were forming over the mountains. "Could be they'll make some progress on that tree house before it rains."

Adam cocked a brow. "Does that mean we'll finally be getting rain?"

Tom nodded. "My knees are telling me so, and they're seldom wrong." That said, he strolled off with a wave.

Soon afterward the two women Jane had been talking to also departed with brochures in hand. She turned to Adam, thinking that he looked more like a businessman today in his dark trousers and light gray knit shirt. Not as polished as the first time she'd laid eyes on him, but polished enough to match the casual yet professional tone of today's fair.

When it came to being in the public eye, the man knew how to strike the right note, that was clear. Whereas she was a long way from feeling at ease in her getup, she was trying her darnedest not to show it.

"Those women who just left may bring in some business," she informed him. "They thought that the, uh, hot tubs were a good idea."

Told you so, the pointed gaze that met hers said as plainly as if he'd spoken the words.

"Then again," she continued, "they were of the opinion that the mirrored wall backing the tubs might be a little much."

"The newlyweds won't think so," he assured her. "At least, not the groom."

Jane lifted one shoulder in a small shrug. "I guess I'll have to take your word for it."

"You do that," he replied calmly.

Had she detected any arrogance in his tone, she'd have kicked him under the table. Accidentally, of course. She'd probably have wound up with sore toes, though. Sandals were no match for boots, she was forced to concede. Not when the target was a strong male shin.

"Hi, Janie," someone said. "Nice to see you."

She recognized the voice before she looked up. A slyness had always underscored most of what came out of Bobby Breen's mouth. She couldn't believe she'd once found it appealing, right along with his blond-haired, blue-eyed, beach-boy looks. Her only defense was that she'd been too young to recognize a love-'em-until-something-better-comes-along type when she saw one.

"Hello, Bobby," she said in a strictly neutral greeting. To display no emotion wasn't hard. She'd stopped feeling anything where Bobby was concerned years ago.

"Long time no see, Janie."

Okay, so she could still feel something. Bobby's continuing to call her "Janie" at this late date irritated her no end.

"How's Belinda?" she asked, a bit more crisply than she'd intended.

Bobby took the reminder that he had a wife in stride. Belinda Montgomery had been one of the most popular girls at Harmony High—and more than attractive enough to have Bobby ditching Jane in a flash when the well-built brunette had turned her eyes his way.

"She's all right," Bobby said. "Put on some weight after the last kid, but then, haven't we all?" He padded a rounded stomach once washboard flat. "All except you, Janie. I don't think you've gained an ounce." His frank stare made a lingering journey from the top of her head to the hands she'd folded on the table. "You look good."

Out of the corner of her eye, she thought she saw Adam's jaw tighten for a second. But she might have been mistaken. Any change in his expression had come and gone too quickly to really tell.

"It's so nice to see you youngsters enjoying the fresh air." For the second time a familiar voice, this one brimming with good cheer, won Jane's attention.

"Hello, Miss Hester," she said, and added a smile to welcome the retired schoolteacher.

Hester Goodbody returned that smile, then aimed her sharp-eyed gaze at Bobby. "I believe your wife could use your help. She's sitting on one of the benches toward the front of the square with a baby and a toddler both crying."

Bobby kept his eyes on Jane. "Hope to see you in town more often." With that he sauntered away, as though in no hurry at all.

"Jerk," she believed she heard Adam mutter. But again she had to conclude that she might be wrong when his expression revealed nothing to back it up.

"How are you, my dear?" Miss Hester asked Jane.

As well as can be expected when I'd rather be back at Glory Ridge doing what I know how to do, Jane thought. "Fine," she said.

Miss Hester's attention fixed on Adam. "As I remember, you were quick on the mark, even in first grade. So I think you'll agree that Jane looks wonderful."

Adam nodded carefully but said nothing.

The elderly woman seemed amused by his cautious agreement. "I'm sure many young men would consider it a treat to be in Jane's company on this beautiful day."

Just then, as if Miss Hester had conjured them, three men approached the table. Jane didn't recognize them, and it turned out that they were visitors to Harmony. They asked several questions about the resort, directing all of them to its owner.

At a particular point in the discussion, Jane's ears caught what sounded like a growl coming from

Adam. She dismissed it in short order, deciding she was probably mistaken one more time.

After all, things were going well. Why in the world would he be growling?

TO GROWL HIS DISPLEASURE had been a mistake. Adam knew that and had to hope no one had picked up on it.

No one besides Hester Goodbody, that is. He hadn't missed the quick look she'd sent his way. He'd done his best to ignore the look, a mix of good-natured humor and wry sympathy. She'd apparently concluded that the green-eyed jealousy monster had bitten him and she was commiserating. It nearly had his teeth clenching in response. He didn't even want to consider the possibility that she could be right.

Luckily, the elderly woman had probably been the only one to notice. The men dancing attendance on Jane certainly hadn't paid him any mind. They'd been too busy focusing on her.

Which shouldn't mean a tinker's damn to you, the voice of reason reminded him.

Trouble was, he wasn't feeling reasonable at the moment. One thing for sure, the good mood he'd started the day with had disappeared.

Adam glanced at Jane, who sat beside him in his rental car. They were headed back to Glory Ridge, the sun low in the afternoon sky and more clouds beginning to roll in. Conversation had ground to a halt a while ago, chiefly because he had little desire to talk enough to keep up his end. What he wanted to do was get back to his cabin, pour himself a short glass of wine and...brood.

Yes, that was precisely what he wanted to do.

Brooding didn't make much sense—hell, it didn't make *any* sense after a day spent watching his promotional ideas prove a hit—but there it was.

"I've got a hunch we're on track to getting some rain at last," Jane said, breaking a long silence.

Adam slowed to negotiate a turn in the winding road leading up the side of the mountain. "Tom Kennedy said his knees were predicting as much."

"Hmm." Jane paused, then went on in the next breath, as though determined to keep another silence at bay. "Curt Bartlett just might get caught in it before he gets back from his hike. He told me yesterday that he planned to be out all day."

The mention of Glory Ridge's latest guest took Adam back to the afternoon Jane had returned with her new look. He had no trouble remembering the appreciative gleam in Bartlett's eyes. No trouble at all, he thought grimly, his hands tightening on the steering wheel of their own accord.

"Do you find anything strange about that guy?" he asked with another glance Jane's way.

She frowned, as though puzzled by his remark. "Curt?"

"Yeah, *Curt.*" That they were chummy enough to be on a first-name basis had Adam's mood slipping even further.

"No, I haven't found anything strange about him," she replied after a moment.

It wasn't just that Bartlett had clearly taken to Jane's new image, Adam told himself. From the moment Bartlett had arrived, something about the guy had put Adam on edge. He wished he knew what. "Goes for a lot of walks in the woods, doesn't he?"

"That's apparently why he came here," Jane said. "The man is obviously an experienced hiker."

"Uh-huh. But what does he do out there all by himself?"

"Whatever he wants to, I suppose."

Adam didn't miss how his passenger was sounding more exasperated by the minute. Although well aware that he was trying her patience, right now he wasn't inclined to care.

"I don't have to worry about *him* getting lost, that's for sure," she added, as though she couldn't resist that little zinger.

"I never got lost," he grumbled, ignoring a twinge that came straight from his conscience over that bending of the truth.

"I never said you did," she pointed out coolly.

She had him there. "I'm just suggesting that appearances can be deceiving. Mr. Outdoorsman might be a case in point. Did he ever tell you what he does for a living?"

"No, and I'm not about to ask him. Guests at Glory Ridge are entitled to their privacy."

He would have liked to argue that point—and couldn't. It didn't sit well with him, though, that if he and Sam weren't there, she'd be alone with someone she knew virtually nothing about. "Privacy is one thing, but you have to be careful."

"I know how to be careful," Jane informed him, clipping the words. She was fast coming to the conclusion that her ears hadn't deceived her back at the fair. Adam could have issued that growl. He certainly appeared to be acting grouchy at the moment.

A heavy silence again descended, one that lasted until they pulled into the resort parking lot. Jane supposed it was fate—or maybe sheer bad luck—that Curt Bartlett tramped out of the woods at the very moment she got out of the car. He waved and started toward her, his well-used backpack settled between his broad shoulders.

"How did it go today?" he asked. Rather than being just polite, he sounded genuinely interested.

"Things went well," she replied. "The business fair seemed to be a big success." A gust of wind sent the full skirt of her flower-strewn dress swirling. She caught it before it whipped up to her waist. But not before a good length of bare leg was exposed. This was why she preferred pants. Skirts could be a pain in the posterior.

And so could hotshot consultants, Jane groused to herself as she caught the scowl that had settled on Adam's face from where he stood steps away, arms crossed over his chest. He gave every indication of viewing the other man in their threesome as public enemy number one.

"I'll see you tomorrow," Adam said, finally speaking and directing that unmistakably terse comment to Jane. Then he turned on the heel of one polished loafer and stalked away.

"He seems a tad upset," Curt drawled.

Jane knew that was putting it mildly. She had to be grateful that the seasoned outdoorsman who was spending good money to stay at Glory Ridge didn't appear to take offense. "It's been a long day," she said by way of explanation, and left it at that.

"But a successful one, you said."

She nodded. "There was a lot of interest in the new plan for the resort."

Curt considered that information. "But will it lead

to real customers down the road?'' he asked. ''I won't deny it's none of my business, but before you go making too many changes around here, it might be smart to think twice about the whole thing.''

It was a natural enough comment, especially coming from someone totally at home in rustic settings—even as rustic a setting as Glory Ridge currently was. But for some reason it had Jane recalling Adam's earlier question.

Do you find anything strange about that guy?

Since she couldn't really say she did, she decided to reserve judgment for the moment. In the end, she groped for a politely noncommittal reply to Curt's remark and left him with the warning that if what was beginning to look more and more like a major storm approaching actually materialized, the electricity might go out.

Curt assured her he'd cope just fine and, having no doubt that he would, Jane beat a swift retreat. The steadily rising wind at her back pushed her along and had her keeping a grip on her skirt.

There was no sign of Adam as she passed Squirrel Hollow cabin. She recalled that Sam was spending the night with Travis, news he'd passed along with unmistakable excitement. Sam's father, she thought with perverse satisfaction, would just have to be grouchy alone. And it served him right.

By the time she reached Pitt's Pride, Jane had come to the firm conclusion that the only person acting strange was Adam.

HE KNEW HE'D behaved like an ass, but there was no room for remorse in his current state. It was past midnight and the only thing Adam could feel was the tension that had hounded him for too many hours to count. The half bottle of wine he'd downed earlier hadn't begun to take the edge off. And then the storm had blown in with a vengeance. The lights had gone out and sleep had proved impossible when he'd discovered that the cabin roof leaked.

Drip...drip...drip.

Water plopped into the large bowl he'd found in a kitchen cabinet with the help of a flashlight. Ever since setting it on the floor beside the bed, he'd been treated to what was turning out to be slow torture.

Drip...drip...drip.

"And where is the woman who put you here, Lassiter?" he grumbled as he stared up at a dark ceiling. "Probably happily asleep with nothing to drive her crazy."

He laced his fingers behind his head, closed his eyes and willed himself to get some rest. He tried the time-honored method of counting sheep, but came up empty. A bid to count the worms he'd lost to a clever trout soon proved a failure, as well. In desperation, he turned one ear into a lumpy pillow and placed another pillow over his head. He still couldn't drown out the sound that was twisting his gut into knots.

Drip...drip...drip.

That tore it!

Adam rolled over, switched on the flashlight he'd placed next to the bed and surged to his feet, determined to take his frustration out on someone. And he knew just who.

"Let's see how she likes doing without sleep," he muttered as he pulled off his sweatpants and pulled on his jeans. He shoved his feet into his boots and shrugged into a denim shirt. He didn't bother to button it. He just grabbed the flashlight and stalked toward the front door.

A steady stream of rain poured down on him as he headed for Pitt's Pride. He'd never been to Jane's cabin, but he knew the general direction and imagined it wouldn't be hard to find. Although half-hidden by the trees surrounding it, he soon caught sight of the building as a jagged bolt of lightning lit the sky. The cabin was smaller than Squirrel Hollow but constructed of the same thick logs.

A few rapid strides took him past the narrow covered porch and up to the door. He didn't hesitate to pound a fist on the well-worn wood. And then he pounded some more until it opened with a quick jerk.

Jane took one look at the person standing on her doorstep and wasted no time in frowning up at him. "What in the world is the mat—"

He cut her off by pushing past her, stomping his way over bare wood. He was steps inside when he whirled and pinned her in the glare of the flashlight. Her face was scrubbed clean, her hair mussed from sleep, and the old navy T-shirt that covered her from neck to knees had nothing to recommend it but the fact that it was dry. The sight of her certainly shouldn't have stirred his libido right along with his temper. But it did.

"I'll tell you what's the matter," he bit out. "The roof of the cabin you were so kind to give me leaks!"

"Oh." She shut the door before again meeting his gaze. "I'm sorry."

"*Sorry?*" He was in no mood to be pacified and knew it showed.

She sighed. "I didn't think that one leaked. It never has before. I'll get it fixed first thing tomorrow."

But he was still considering the words *that one.* "Do you mean some of the other cabins leak?"

She shrugged. "Most of them, as a matter of fact. And in case you haven't noticed, mine is hardly an exception."

That statement, ripe with irony, had Adam looking around him. Only then he did he see the coffee cans randomly placed on the floor. And only then did his ears pick up the sound that had driven him crazy earlier, magnified several times over.

Drip…drip…drip.

"Jeez, how do you stand it?" he asked, whipping the flashlight back to Jane.

"I'm used to it."

For some reason that quietly blunt statement had his temper rising to new heights. "You shouldn't be living like this."

She crossed her arms. "I plan to get the roof fixed as soon as the other cabins are done. Until then, a little water won't hurt me."

He closed the gap between them with a quick stretch of his long legs and curled a hand around her upper arm. He wanted to shake her, but the feel of her soft skin under his palm shook him. No, he didn't want to shake her, he admitted to himself as they stared at each other, eyes locked.

He just wanted her. Badly.

It had been eating away at him, he realized, ever since he'd kissed her. And now he needed more than kisses. A lot more.

Something must have showed in his gaze, because

her own widened. She cleared her throat. "I can't do anything about that leak now. If you can go back and put up with it for tonight—"

"I don't want to go back," he said, his voice nearly as quiet and even more blunt than hers had been earlier. He was through fighting the attraction, he thought. Time to lay things on the line. Then, what happened next would be her decision.

"I want to stay here—with you."

Jane swallowed hard but said nothing, her expression frozen.

He released her and took a step back. "But whether I stay or go is up to you."

A crack of thunder split the silence as he kept his hands at his sides and waited for her answer. Water dripped around them for what might have been the longest minute of his life before she whispered two halting words that sent his blood racing through his veins.

"Don't...go."

Chapter Nine

Don't go. Had she actually said that?

Yes, she must have, Jane concluded when Adam strode forward and wrapped an arm around her waist to quickly tug her to him, as though he had no doubt his embrace would be welcomed.

Was she sorry she'd said it?

No, not a whit, she thought as his mouth came down on hers. If she was going to have regrets, they would have to come later. Right now, everything inside her was urging her to forge ahead, sure that she and the man she'd never dreamed of having for a lover—even for one stormy night—were on a fast track to making that a reality.

They would be lovers. And soon.

As if he fully agreed with that prediction, Adam kissed her as he had before, long and hard and deep, until they both needed to breathe. She was still filling her lungs full when he looked down at her, once again staring straight into her eyes.

"Bedroom." The single word, issued in a husky voice, sent her heart fluttering.

"That way," she said, nodding toward the back of the cabin.

With a strong arm still wound around her waist and his other hand holding the flashlight, he picked her right up off her bare feet and wasted no time in reaching his objective, despite the coffee cans he had to dodge along the way.

He set the flashlight on the dresser and left it lit to cast a soft glow over the room. Then his attention centered on the old pine bed he'd hauled her out of with a fist to the door.

"It doesn't have a five-star mattress," she said as lightly as she could manage with her breath still threatening to catch in her throat. "Or even two stars."

That had his mouth slanting up at a corner. "We'll make do."

She nodded slowly. "I guess we will."

His crooked smile widened. "To avoid risking a chill, I suppose the first thing to do is get out of these wet clothes."

"Mmm-hmm." Moisture soaked the front of her T-shirt from being plastered from shoulder to knee against his rain-drenched body, yet the last thing she felt was chilled.

He shrugged out of his black shirt, revealing a wide expanse of hair-darkened skin that she'd by no means forgotten from her first sight of it. After dropping the shirt on the floor, where it landed with a soggy plop, he cocked a brow. "You're wet, too."

And he expected her to do something about it; that was clear. But she wasn't ready. The bald truth was, with events fast proceeding, her nerves were beginning to do a tap dance up her spine.

"I'm not as wet as you are," she pointed out.

"Okay, I'll buy that," he told her.

But the glint in his eyes said he recognized a delaying tactic when he heard one. Looking not in the least self-conscious, he toed off his boots, lowered his zipper gingerly past the very male bulge beneath it and let his soaked Levi's fall to the floor.

She wouldn't have been too surprised to find him wearing fancy silk underwear. But he wasn't wearing any, period.

And it was as plain as a fence post that he was...ready.

"We may have to get creative before this is over," he said, his voice turning even deeper, huskier, than before.

That statement had her gaze snapping back up to meet his. "Creative?" she ventured cautiously.

"I didn't come prepared for this."

She caught his drift and had to be grateful that her sister had provided a solution. Thankfully, they wouldn't have to resort to too much creativity—which *she* wasn't prepared for.

She pointed to her dresser. "You'll find what you need in that honey jar."

For a moment he just stared at her. "You're full of surprises, aren't you?"

He didn't wait for a reply. He just turned away, providing her with a fine view of a tight male backside, and retrieved a foil packet from the jar. Then he approached her with slow steps. "That T-shirt really has to come off."

She stood her ground but didn't move a muscle. He was the one who finally dealt with the problem, and her makeshift nightwear had scarcely joined his clothes on the floor when she found herself on the bed, flat on her back, with a long, lean, warm and naked man half-stretched out over her.

"I guess you're in a hurry," she said with all the calm she could muster.

His expression sobered as he settled his weight on his elbows. "I'd be kidding both of us if I said I could string this out indefinitely. I can't, not this time."

In the end, her pride came to her rescue. She'd told him not to go and she wouldn't drag her heels now. Reaching up, she wrapped her arms around his neck. "I don't want to string it out, either."

But they both had to wait for her body to accept him after he applied protection and pressed forward, easing his way into her tightness. At last the intimate connection was accomplished, and he felt...better than anything she'd ever felt before, Jane decided, sighing her approval. It wasn't long before she gave herself up to that feeling as he established a steady rhythm.

It was so easy, so unaccountably and undeniably easy, to lose herself in him.

Above her, Adam tightened his jaw in an effort not to surrender to the release his body was demanding, had been demanding almost from the moment Jane had invited him to stay with her. He knew he should have given her time, should have at least made an effort at foreplay. Truth be told, he couldn't remember when he'd been this eager to get to the main event with little pause along the way.

Must be all that fresh air, Lassiter.

But even as that wry thought hit, he knew there was more to it. Much of it had to do not just with himself but who he was with and how her small, neat body felt under his. *Lush* would never describe her. *Petite* was far more accurate. But she made an impact, nonetheless.

The assault on his senses threatened to wipe out every last scrap of his control. If he wasn't careful he'd leave her wanting, Adam realized as he picked up the pace. That thought and that thought alone kept him from giving in, and he couldn't help but be grateful for his restraint when Jane's breathing began to change, becoming almost as hard and fast as his own.

"I think we're almost there," he told her in a rough whisper at her ear, hoping to heaven it was true.

"Adam." She clutched him tighter, tangling her legs with his, the same legs he—and another man, damn him!—had gotten more than a glimpse of due to a gust of wind. Thankfully, the even bigger eyeful he'd gotten just minutes ago after tugging her T-shirt over her head had been private. Trouble was, he hadn't taken the time to see enough, not nearly enough—something he would rectify later, he promised himself.

Adam's thoughts scattered as Jane shuddered in his arms. Her soft cry was music to his ears. Now he knew he could let himself go, throw off the self-imposed chains that bound him. And find some ease.

Seconds later, he convulsed with a low shout...and found a small piece of paradise.

He didn't want to come back to earth, resisted it as long as he could. He wanted to stay where he was with his nose buried in soft, short strands of hair that smelled like an apple orchard. But the woman under him would probably appreciate the chance to breathe.

With a small groan, he raised his upper body and discovered himself being viewed by a pair of hazel eyes that seemed larger even without any hint of makeup. He dropped a brief kiss down on a small, straight nose. "How are you feeling?"

"Good," Jane replied after a beat. But her attempt at a casual tone didn't quite succeed.

Well, if that was the way she wanted to handle the matter, Adam thought, he supposed it was the lady's choice. There was no way, though, that he was forgetting how she'd shuddered and cried out in his arms. There'd been nothing casual about that.

"I need to visit the bathroom," he said, keeping his own voice deliberately even. With that, he slowly pushed away, rose to his feet, grabbed up the flashlight and left the room. Small as the cabin was, the bathroom wasn't hard to find, and he was back in a matter of minutes.

Jane was still in bed, he discovered. The worn ivory bedspread was pulled up to her neck and her eyes were closed. He leaned a shoulder against one side of the bedroom doorway, glanced around him and found two more coffee cans standing on the floor on the far side of the room. He'd been too occupied with other things to pay much attention to the water leaking from the ceiling. Now he heard it again loud and clear.

Drip...drip...drip.

The flashlight chose that moment to die. He set it on the floor, threaded his way through the dark until he reached the bed, and slid under the bedspread. "Asleep?" he asked in a low murmur.

"No." Jane shifted slightly, turning toward him.

"I don't think I'll be able to sleep with the on-going water torture."

"It just takes some getting used to."

"Hmm. Could be, but I'll probably have to keep myself occupied for a while." With that, he ducked his head under the covers. As if they had radar, his lips homed in on a soft yet firm breast. He didn't miss the little moans it won him. And he didn't stop there, just continued his way downward, inch by inch.

"Good grief," Jane said, her moans giving way to a gasp.

He chuckled against the silky skin of her flat belly. "It's time," he told her, "to experiment."

EXPERIMENTING DIDN'T BEGIN to describe what happened. The man had turned her right on her ear, Jane had to admit the next morning as she emptied the coffee cans scattered around the cabin living room. She'd already dealt with those in the bedroom while Adam slept on. Thanks to her internal clock, she'd already been awake when the first birds had started chirping to welcome the dawn of a sunny day.

Jane glanced out the bare front window. If not for the still-damp clothing—both hers and Adam's—that she'd rescued from the floor and draped over the porch railing to dry, the scene would look pretty much as though the storm had never happened. But it had happened. And so had the rest of last night.

With the coffee cans empty and stacked at the side of the kitchen sink, Jane brushed her palms on the cutoff jeans she'd tugged on after her shower and began to put Sweet Pea's breakfast together. She soon found the skunk patiently waiting at the bottom of the porch stairs.

"Okay, so I'm late again," she admitted. "I had some things to take care of, thanks to that downpour we had."

Sweet Pea sniffed her food and started to dig in.

"Oh, yeah. Easy for you to eat," Jane said. "You didn't wake up with butterflies in *your* stomach." Which she had, she couldn't deny as she drew in a cool, steadying breath of rain-washed air.

She wasn't used to starting her morning with a naked man in her bed. Flat on his stomach he'd been, with his half of the bedspread kicked right off of him and a luscious length of sheer maleness on display. She'd waged an inner war for a few silent moments, her eyes ready to continue looking their fill and her nerves voting that she get going and put some clothes on before he woke up. Since there'd been no one around to impress with her courage, she'd gone along with her nerves.

"You, on the other hand," she told her companion, "don't have those kind of problems. All you have to worry about is making sure your bed under the porch stays dry."

"Do you always talk to skunks?" a low voice asked.

Jane turned and found Adam standing on the other side of the screen door. Moisture flecked his dark hair, she noted, as if he'd followed her example and showered. She also couldn't help noticing that he wore a towel hitched at his hips—and nothing else.

She inhaled another steadying breath and crossed her arms over the front of a cotton tank top once light blue but now almost white from many washings. "Well, I didn't have you to talk to, did I?" she asked, mustering an arch tone. "You were dead to the world while I was up and doing things around here."

His lips quirked. "Guilty as charged. But then, I got a lot of exercise last night."

Boy, had he ever. And he knew what he'd been doing. When it came to making love, Adam Lassiter was no amateur, that was for sure. In fact, Jane had to acknowledge that he could well be considered an expert. Certainly he had far more experience in that area than she did.

Her bare feet were becoming cold from standing on wood that had yet to feel the rising sun's rays. Her cheeks, however, were warming with the way he ran his gaze over her slowly and thoroughly, as if she hadn't bothered to put on any clothes. She wasn't finding any comfort in that lingering appraisal, although she tried not to show it.

"Your shirt and jeans should be dry soon," she said.

He met her gaze. "I'm in no hurry to get dressed."

Great, Jane thought with an inner sigh, knowing his lack of clothing only multiplied her discomfort. Again she did her best to be flippant. "Wouldn't want you to risk getting a chill."

His deep chuckle was as sexy a sound as she'd ever heard. "I don't think I'm coming down with the sniffles, but maybe you could feed me to bolster my resistance."

"I could," Jane agreed. At least it would give her hands something to do. Right now they wanted to twist themselves behind her back. "I only make simple food," she warned.

This time his chuckle was ripe with dry humor. "I didn't expect Eggs Benedict."

"Eggs what?"

"Never mind. Scrambled will do."

She fed him, and even managed to swallow some eggs and toast herself.

Sipping his coffee, he glanced at the old percolator on the stove, the same type of coffeemaker all the cabins sported. "I still haven't figured out how to produce anything this drinkable with that contraption."

She had to smile. "Even with fancy beans?"

"Even with those," he agreed. "What's the secret?"

She leaned back in her chair and shrugged. "Practice."

He pushed his empty plate away as his eyes gleamed. "I'd say you're right. Practice is the key to anything."

Something told her he was no longer talking about food. She cleared her throat. "I guess so," she agreed. Back to needing something to do, she rose, grabbed up their plates and put them in the sink. She didn't even hear him come up behind her until his lips were at her ear.

"I want to practice."

She was the one who could use some practice in what he was proposing, not him. But she wasn't going to say so. Heck, she probably didn't have to. Nevertheless, she was the woman he'd wanted last night, she reminded herself. And he still wanted her. That much was clear.

He was giving her the choice yet again, she realized. And the blunt truth was, she wanted him, too.

She turned, tipped her face up and placed her small hands on his broad shoulders. "I suppose," she said with a wry lift of her brow, "a little practice wouldn't hurt."

IT DIDN'T. Far from it. In fact, making love to Jane felt just as great as it had last night, Adam reflected with satisfaction. With his pulse still attempting to slow its pace after another enthusiastic round of intimate activities, he considered himself a contented man as he ran a hand over a silky smooth hip. Of course, he had to dig under the covers to do it, because Jane had once more yanked the bedspread up to her shoulders the minute she'd had the chance. Her modesty was beginning to intrigue him. Somehow the primness didn't mesh with her usual bravado.

Then again, he hadn't forgotten how her body had had to be coaxed into accepting him their first time together. She didn't regularly invite men to her bed, that much was obvious. And, despite the fact that she could make a man think twice about getting on her bad side, she was delicate. That delicacy had been right before his eyes, but he hadn't really seen it, not until now.

Adam lifted his head, propped it on an elbow and stared down the length of Jane's stretched-out form. Only her bare feet were visible to the eye, sticking out from the covers. Ten dainty toes looked tasty enough to nibble on, and with more pressing concerns taken care of for the moment, he was far from reluctant to do it. Or...

A grin curved Adam's mouth as he hit on a plan for Jane's toes—one he was more than ready to put into action. "Be right back," he murmured. Although her eyes were closed, he knew she wasn't asleep.

"Mmm-hmm," she murmured in return.

He went to the bathroom, dealt with the necessities and returned to the bedroom. Rather than heading straight back to Jane, he made a detour to the dresser, where he'd recalled seeing something on one of his earlier trips for the foil packets kept there. He picked up a small bottle shaded a creamy pink and returned to the bed, where he sat on an edge of the mattress.

Only when he took one of Jane's feet in a light grasp and set it in his lap did she peek at him. "In case you haven't noticed," she told him on a yawn, "I haven't been on my feet enough lately for them to require a rub."

"Glad to hear it, because I plan on painting your toenails."

That got her eyes open in a hurry. "You are not."

"I am." When she tried to yank her foot away, he held on tight. "This polish is going to spill all over if you don't lie still," he told her calmly.

She frowned at him. "I don't need my toes painted."

"They'll match your fingernails," he pointed out—reasonably, in his opinion.

She tightened the hand resting at her side into a fist his own would have dwarfed. "I didn't have to have my fingernails painted, either," she grumbled—more to herself than to him, he imagined, because he scarcely caught the words.

Deciding just to get on with it, he dipped the brush in the polish and started with her big toe—*big* hardly describing it. He figured his tactics were working when she didn't argue anymore. Either that or she was too busy mulling over the joys of kicking him out at the earliest opportunity.

Whatever the case, silence reigned while he finished one foot. He started on the second, then paused in his task as something occurred to him. It was another puzzle that didn't quite fit the picture where this woman was concerned.

"Mind if I ask why you keep protection in that honey jar?" he said, making the question casual.

She blew out a breath. "It was the first place I could think of to dump the things."

He thought about that for a minute. "I'm getting the impression you didn't buy them."

"No, Ellen did. For my birthday. In October."

"Last October?"

"No, *this* October." She rolled her eyes. "It's a long story."

"Must be," he agreed. And damn if he wasn't getting more intrigued by the minute. "Was that all your sister got you?"

She gave her head a quick shake. "You wouldn't believe what she—" Jane came to a dead halt. "Never mind," she added after a beat, as though deciding she'd said too much.

Adam let the matter go, but it didn't stop him from wondering. He finished her second foot, taking his time, and finally closed the bottle with a quick twist. He'd done a passable job, he mused, viewing his handiwork. Jane's toes looked even more tempting than before.

"Maybe this wasn't such a good idea," he admitted ruefully as memories of his frustration with some of yesterday's events came back to him. "You were getting plenty of attention at the fair without your toes being painted. That Bobby guy, for instance.''

''Ancient history,'' Jane said after a moment, as though Bobby Whoever didn't matter a whit to her.

But there had been something between them at one time. Adam was quick to reach that conclusion. Not that it was any of his business, he reminded himself.

''Then there were all those other guys who wanted to get to know you better—a lot better.''

Jane met that statement with another frown, one that seemed more puzzled than annoyed. ''If you mean some of the people I was talking to about the resort—''

''I mean the men who couldn't have cared less about the resort. They had their sights set on you.''

Her jaw dropped. ''You're kidding.''

''I'm not, believe me.''

But she didn't believe him, Adam realized in the next breath as her expression changed from amazement to irony and she all but shouted, *Get real!* This time modesty had nothing to do with it, he recognized. Her reaction was no politely humble protest. She was simply sure he was wrong.

Why? he had to ask himself.

A possible answer appeared to him as the memory of Tom Kennedy's story about a far younger Jane surfaced. The little girl and the father who'd ignored her in favor of his other, prettier, daughter. The same little girl who'd squared her shoulders and tagged along after them. Had she ever won any measure of praise from him? And if not, what would its lack do to the girl who'd grown up without it?

It would produce the person Jane Pitt had become. Self-assured on the outside, but not nearly so confident down deep, certainly not when it came to her womanly abilities to win a man's attention. All at once Adam was as positive of that as he'd ever been of anything.

"If your father had been around to see you at the fair," he ventured, careful to keep his voice even, "he'd probably have recognized that those guys had more than business in mind."

Jane snorted. "Not a chance."

"Because he wouldn't notice the changes you made?"

"They weren't that big a deal," she replied with a small shrug. "I just looked a little...different."

"You looked damn good," Adam countered. Bluntness might be the only way to get his point across. "If the man who fathered you wouldn't be able to see that, I'd put it down to sheer blindness. And maybe it's time to stop looking at yourself through his eyes."

He'd hit a nerve. He knew it when Jane met his comment with a glare. He'd ticked her off, but right now he didn't care. "Until that happens," he added, staring her straight in the eye, "you may never be the person you can be."

With that he got up, stepped over to the dresser to put the bottle of pink polish back where he'd found it and headed for the bedroom door. *Might as well leave before she kicks you out, Lassiter,* he told himself, grabbing up his boots.

"It'll be time to pick up Sam soon," he said. "I'll talk to you later."

A tense silence ripe with undercurrents greeted that remark, as though Jane had no intention of talking to him any time soon. But he wouldn't apologize, he reflected grimly as he walked through the bed-room doorway naked as the day he'd been born. After all, he'd spoken no more than he considered the truth.

Muttering a soft oath, he let the screen door slam behind him on his way out, then dressed on the porch and shoved his feet into his boots. His long legs made quick work of the short distance to Squirrel Hollow cabin. He was steps from the building and deep in his thoughts when he caught sight of something that had him stopping in his tracks.

Curt Bartlett, once again hefting a large backpack between his shoulders, stood a few yards away. Half turned toward Adam but looking straight ahead, he seemed to be studying a point off in the distance, his gazed narrowed in calculation, as though he were weighing and measuring something in his mind. Seconds passed before he headed for the woods and was soon lost in the trees.

Adam scrubbed a hand consideringly over the night's growth of dark stubble on his jaw. Something was telling him that Bartlett intended more than a casual hike, and it fit right in with his earlier intuition that the guy was acting strange.

He could be dead wrong, of course. Nevertheless, the memory of what he'd seen dogged him as he took his second shower of the morning, shaved and dressed again in clothes that hadn't spent the night on the floor. Finally he decided that it wouldn't hurt to do some checking. He retrieved a phone number from his Palm Pilot and dialed it on his cell phone. Minutes later he disconnected the call, feeling easier in his mind for having asked an acquaintance of his—a computer whiz with an uncanny ability to ferret out information not always readily available—to attempt a little digging on Glory Ridge's newest guest.

Adam heaved a gusty sigh and headed out to pick up Sam. As to how he'd left the situation with Jane, he felt a long way from easy, much less content. But he still wasn't sorry, even though she was probably cursing him right this minute.

"DOUBLE-DARN AND BLAST the man!"

Jane repeated the words she'd already ground out too many times to count in the past several hours. The first time was when she'd hopped out of bed, every bit of her anger directed at the person who'd left her minutes earlier without so much as a backward glance.

Now she was knee-deep in a weekly cleaning, preferring to spend the day at her cabin rather than going down to the office and risk running into *him*. She'd stopped by there briefly to give the crew renovating the cabins a new list of priorities. First, fix the roof at Squirrel Hollow cabin—soon to be renamed Sweet Seclusion, heaven help her—then do the same at Pitt's Pride.

She had to admit that her hotshot consultant was right on one score. There was no reason for her to live with the leaks any longer than she had to, and there was no mistaking the fact that another downpour was due tonight. Jane didn't have to listen to the radio forecast to know it.

The same towering clouds that had built up by late yesterday afternoon were rolling in once again. The wind had already started to pick up. Rain, with its full share of thunder and lightning, probably wouldn't be far behind, and the electricity just might go out for the second time in twenty-four hours.

But tonight no royally teed-off guest would be banging on her door. Tonight she wouldn't find a tall, dark and rain-drenched man with a dangerous glint in his eye standing on her doorstep.

Tonight she'd be sleeping alone.

Which suited her just fine, Jane told herself. She shoved the rag mop she was using to clean the bathroom floor into a bucket of soapy water, jerked it out again and bent to wring it. Putting her muscles into the task wasn't hard. She just imagined her hands were wrapped around Adam Lassiter's neck.

"Some lover," she griped out loud. "He might know what he's doing when it comes to the main event, but the intermission could use some work. You think he'd have learned sometime in his thirty-plus years to keep his nose out of his bed partner's personal affairs and his opinions to himself."

The floor done, Jane set the mop aside and began to scrub the bathroom sink. She didn't want to consider the fact that only hours had passed since Adam was standing in the same spot she now stood. She didn't want to think about him showering in her small tub and hitching one of her threadbare towels at his hips. She didn't want to recall the sight of him seated across from her at the breakfast table, his damp hair hanging over his forehead, giving a roguish cast to his features.

Most of all, she didn't want to remember the blunt statement he'd issued shortly before leaving: *Maybe it's time to stop looking at yourself through his eyes.*

Trouble was, she couldn't seem to block the words out.

Slowly, she raised her head and studied her face in the mirror over the sink.

The face Adam had said she was seeing through Owen Pitt's eyes. He didn't know how cold those eyes had sometimes been when they'd landed on her. Deep down, she could still feel the chill.

Jane reached up a hand and scraped it through her hair. Every short strand fell back into place in a way it never had before Ellen had gotten her hands on it.

Okay, so her hair did look better, maybe a lot better than it had before, she admitted. Her skin looked better, too. The facial, plus the moisturizer she'd promised to use, made it seem smoother.

Had those men at the fair she'd been dead sure were only interested in the resort been interested in her, instead? She still didn't think so.

Because your father wouldn't?

She blew out a breath as that niggling question rattled through her brain. She knew who'd put it there.

"Blast the man," she said one more time, scrubbing the sink with renewed vigor. Quiet minutes passed before something again pulled her gaze to the mirror. She took another long look, one that eventually had her frowning more in thought than irritation.

Could the man she'd taken into her bed last night, the same man she'd been cursing up, down and sideways most of the day, somehow be right?

Chapter Ten

Adam ran his fingers over the computer keys and tried to keep his mind on his project. In addition to the ad he'd just placed in a prominent magazine geared to the bridal market, Glory Ridge needed another way to reach potential customers who had never heard of the Harmony region, much less visited there. The Web site he was creating was a means to achieve that goal. It was important enough to deserve his full attention, certainly. Trouble was, his thoughts were set on wandering to the woman who'd been making herself scarce ever since he'd left her with something to reflect on.

Three days had passed without his getting much more than a glimpse of her. Mostly, he'd seen her off in the distance with the crew renovating the cabins. The decision had apparently been made to fix all the roofs before doing any more painting. A good choice, Adam had to allow, given that torrential downpours during the nighttime hours had become the norm rather than the exception. So far the electricity hadn't gone out again, but whether it would was up for grabs.

Fortunately, he'd found the flashlight he'd left at

Pitt's Pride lying outside his cabin door, batteries replaced. But there'd been no sign of the person who'd left it. Glory Ridge's owner knew how to put her small feet to good use when she wanted to keep out of sight; that was clear.

The whole thing was getting to him, Adam had to admit. Besides finding it difficult to keep his brain on business, his body was nowhere near satisfied after the one night he'd spent with Jane. Truth be told, he missed her—and in a way that went beyond the purely physical, sheer honesty had him conceding. But he still wasn't ready to apologize, even if he'd been able to pin her down long enough to accomplish that.

To top it all off, and only adding to his growing frustration, the recurring dream he'd experienced yet again on his first night at Glory Ridge had haunted his sleep for the past couple of nights. As usual, he'd be striding down a strange corridor and opening a series of doors, to find only blank space awaiting him on the other side. It left him with an empty feeling, one that reached deep inside him.

What the devil did it all mean? he had to ask himself one more time. An answer continued to elude him, and he was relieved to shove thoughts of the increasingly disturbing dream aside as his cell phone rang.

He hoped it meant some news on Bartlett. That matter had been bothering him, as well. Either the guy really was nothing more than an avid vacation hiker, or... Well, that remained to be seen.

"Lassiter here," he said, replying in his usual fashion.

"Hello, Adam," a soft, well-cultured voice greeted him.

He had no trouble recognizing the caller.

"Hello, Ariel."

"How are you?" It was a polite question.

"I'm fine," he said in an equally polite response. They'd both agreed that maintaining a friendly relationship after the divorce was a top priority with a child to consider. "I imagine you want to talk to Sam."

Ariel hesitated a moment, then said, "Actually, I'd like to talk to you."

He didn't miss the way her tone had sobered. "Sounds serious," he said.

Serious enough, in fact, to have him recalling a comment Sam had made during their initial drive up to Glory Ridge. Something about his mother "not sounding so good" when he'd spoken to her on the phone that morning. At the time, Adam hadn't thought much of it, and Sam had phoned Ariel more than once since visiting the resort, with no alarms raised. Nevertheless...

He frowned. "Are you all right, I mean healthwise?" More of that conversation was coming back to him, including Sam's news that his mother had gained some weight—not a typical sign of illness, surely. *But then, you're no doctor, Lassiter.*

"I'm as healthy as always," Ariel assured him. "I just happen to be...pregnant."

Adam's frown disappeared. Yes, that certainly explained a few things, he thought wryly.

"With twins," Ariel added in the next breath.

He leaned back in his chair. "No kidding."

"It was just confirmed this week." She paused

before going on. "Darren and I have been looking forward to having a child together, but this is a little overwhelming, I must admit."

"It could have been triplets," he pointed out dryly.

Her light laugh seemed a bit forced. "Don't even joke about that. Having two newborns to take care of is enough."

"You'll manage."

"Yes, but…"

Something told Adam that *but* was the reason for her call. Ariel had a knack for tiptoeing around a subject. Some would call it a talent for diplomacy, one that probably served her well in dealing with the upper crust in Boston.

She also knew how to employ the precise amount of polite flattery to win a person over. In fact, she'd used it to maximum effect on him when they'd met on one of his business trips shortly after he opened his consulting firm. His parents had received much the same treatment on meeting her for the first time and had readily welcomed Ariel as a potential daughter-in-law.

Her family, on the other hand, had made it clear—in the most courteous way possible, of course—that while the elder Lassiters also traveled in society circles and were descended from hardy pioneer stock, their son really wasn't quite good enough for Ariel, whose own ancestors could be traced back to the days of the Boston Tea Party and the Revolutionary War.

They had married anyway. And then divorced several years later, after both finally admitted it had been a mistake. The best thing to come from that marriage was the child they'd created. Fortunately, he and Ariel had always been in total agreement on that subject.

When he'd heard of her remarriage to someone sure to be more acceptable to her family, he could only wish her well. And he still did. He just wished she'd get to the point.

"How about taking a deep breath and telling me why you called," he suggested calmly. "I have a hunch that it isn't just to pass along the news that your household is set to increase by two."

"No, it's more than that." Again she hesitated, but only for an instant. "It's about Sam."

Her sober tone returned with those last words. And again it had Adam frowning, more in puzzlement than concern this time. "Sam's doing fine."

"I know he is," she acknowledged. "At first, he didn't seem very eager to spend the summer at this resort in the woods, but every time I talk to him he sounds more and more enthusiastic. I think he enjoys being with you."

Adam had to hope it was true, that it wasn't just Glory Ridge and the chance to experience a far different lifestyle that had sparked that enthusiasm. He'd been reluctant to push the issue, to prod Sam into saying how he felt, even after they'd gotten lost together and found a new understanding. Wait for the right moment, he'd been telling himself. The summer wasn't over.

"So," Ariel continued, "since things appear to be going so well, I wanted to suggest that Sam might benefit from spending more time with you."

Adam's frown deepened. "I'm keeping him until he has to fly back to start school," he reminded her.

"Yes, but..."

That last hesitation did it. All of a sudden, his patience was history. "Just spit it out, Ariel."

Apparently taking his advice for once, she abandoned diplomacy and issued a frank question. "How would you feel about Sam's staying with you most of the year and spending his summers with me?"

Adam straightened sharply in his seat. He didn't have to watch his brows shoot halfway up his forehead to realize they had.

"A reversal of the custody agreement," he said slowly, measuring out the words. "Is that what you're suggesting?"

She confirmed it in the next breath. "Yes. Of course, it goes without saying that I wouldn't be suggesting it at all if he didn't sound so good. But since he does, and considering my pregnancy and the coming twins, well, I at least wanted to see how you felt about it."

Adam didn't have to think twice to reach a decision. After years of being primarily a long-distance father, the more time he could spend with his son, the better.

The real question was, how Sam would feel about it.

"TWINS!" Sam's eyes went as round as saucers. "Mom's gonna have *two* babies?"

Adam nodded from his seat beside Sam on their cabin porch steps. "Two," he confirmed.

"Boy, I didn't even know she was having one."

No, an eight-year-old wouldn't recognize the signs, Adam thought. "I told her you'd call her tonight. She wants to talk to you. Right now, though, there's something I'd like to discuss.''

Adam wondered how to phrase what he had to say. He didn't have to grope for words often. They usually came easily—a talent that seemed to have deserted him. Still, he was glad Ariel had agreed with his suggestion that he be the first to broach the subject with Sam. He was here to gauge his son's reaction; she wasn't. It was as simple as that.

What was nowhere near simple was deciding on the best approach to take. In the end, he just waded in.

''The thing is, once the babies show up, your mother's going to be pretty busy. One baby can be a handful, because a baby takes a lot of care at first. Two will take twice as much care.''

Sam mulled that over for a minute, looking off into the lush green woods. ''I suppose.''

''She won't be able to spend as much time with you as she has in the past,'' Adam pointed out with quiet candor. ''So, under the circumstances, she and I were wondering if you'd like to spend more time with me.''

Sam's startled gaze flew to meet his. Adam didn't need perfect vision to see a host of questions there. He just hoped he had the right answers. ''That means you would be with me during the school year and go back to Boston in the summertime.''

When Sam continued to silently stare at him, Adam decided to just keep going. ''We wouldn't be staying at my condo,'' he said, deliberately maintaining a casual tone. He'd already given the matter enough thought since Ariel's call to be certain that new living arrangements were in order. The condo was fine for him, but it was no place to raise a growing child.

"I'd buy a house," he explained, "maybe in Scottsdale so we'd be closer to your grandparents." Lawrence and Doris Lassiter might like their society friends, but they loved their grandson. They'd be thrilled to have him living in the area. Adam knew that without a doubt.

"We couldn't stay here?" Sam asked haltingly, aiming another look around him.

"I'm afraid not." Adam also had no doubts on that score, even though his business was portable. As convenient as his office location was, he didn't need to work out of Phoenix. With modern technology and the fact that all his current clients were based west of the Mississippi, his own home base could be almost anywhere in the western half of the country. Almost anywhere, but not here.

It wasn't the business, he knew. It was him.

Down deep, he was still the man who'd come to Glory Ridge weeks ago, all decked out in his dressed-for-success best. Exchanging a well-tailored suit and imported leather wingtips for casual denim and sturdy boots hadn't changed that. Neither, in the end, had watching, and undeniably admiring, his son's ability to adapt to a new environment.

Not even working long hours side by side with a woman so much a part of this place, not even spending a stormy night making love to her—not even wanting badly to make love to her again—altered the fact that he was still a man who felt far more at home in far different surroundings. Everything came down to one unmistakable truth.

He still didn't belong here.

"But we're not leaving yet," he told Sam, mustering a deliberately bracing tone. "You'll get to help finish that tree house and play in it. We'll do some more fishing, too. And when we do have to leave, you can either go back to Boston or stay with me. Your mother and I have agreed that the decision should be yours."

Although Ariel was clearly feeling overwhelmed at the moment, she hadn't hesitated to make it plain that she loved her son and would welcome him back if that was his choice. But would her new husband—Darren, the banker—be as welcoming? If so, she'd neglected to say as much, Adam thought, recalling their conversation.

And maybe, just maybe, that was the crux of the matter.

It was time, he decided, to get some answers. Lord knows, he'd been wondering about this subject long enough. "Sam, how do you get along with your stepfather?"

Though Adam asked the question quietly, it won Sam's attention in a hurry. He looked at his father, then looked away just as swiftly. "Okay, I guess."

Adam propped his forearms on his knees. "'Okay' doesn't sound that good to me." He linked his fingers when he wanted to fist his hands at the thought of anyone hurting his child. "Is he ever mean to you?"

"No." The reply was quick and firm enough to indicate Sam meant it. "He even helps me with my homework sometimes, and other stuff. It's just…"

"Just what?" Adam prompted gently at the hesitation.

"It's not the same with him and me like it is with

some of my friends and their dads. Ever since he and Mom got married, it's like he never wanted me— *really* wanted me—around.'' Sam slid another look his father's way and swallowed hard, as though gathering his courage, before he spoke again. ''And I wasn't sure you really wanted me, either.''

God, how could he not be sure? The question rang in Adam's mind before logic reminded him that while his son could plainly adapt to new surroundings, being forced to cope with divorce at such a young age, no matter how amiable a break it had been, was bound to leave him vulnerable.

''I want you,'' Adam said, meeting his son's gaze, his words soft yet rough with a surge of gut-wrenching emotion he couldn't begin to stem. ''From the first minute I saw you on the day you were born, I loved you. You were so small back then, and all I could think about was watching you grow up to be the great boy you are.''

He had to clear his throat against a sudden tightness before he could go on. ''I care about you more than I could ever tell you, and I always will, trust me.''

Trust. He could see the beginnings forming in gray eyes so much like his own as the boy beside him swallowed for a second time. Silent seconds passed before Sam slowly rose to his feet. And then, in the next breath, he launched himself straight into his father's arms.

''I want to stay with you, Dad,'' he said with a hitch in his voice as Adam caught him close.

''Then you will,'' Adam replied, his own voice none too steady. ''We'll go back to Boston together for a short visit after the twins arrive so you can meet them and start to get acquainted, but you'll stay with me until next summer.''

For a long moment they simply hugged each other, and that was how Jane found them, locked in a hearty embrace, when she came around a bend in the gravel path and stopped in her tracks at the sight meeting her gaze. Both her eyes and her instincts told her that something important had just occurred.

Even though she'd spent the past few hours gearing herself up to see Adam, she thought about quietly departing before they noticed her. Then the grip they had on each other loosened and Sam looked her way.

''Hey, Jane! Wait till I tell you what happened.'' He glanced at his father, as though seeking permission, and at Adam's nod, Sam wasted no time in heading toward her as fast as his now woods-scuffed running shoes would take him.

''My mom's gonna have a baby,'' he said in an eager rush. ''No, she's gonna have *two* of them. And I get to stay with my dad in a new house he's going to buy close to Gram and Granddad Lassiter.''

It took Jane a moment to absorb that information and another to find her voice. ''That's…great.''

Sam certainly seemed to think so. Despite a thin sheen of moisture making his eyes overbright, he was all smiles. ''Yeah, but before that I get to help Travis finish the tree house and do some more fishing.'' He rubbed a hand under his nose. ''I need to dig up more worms.''

Because she suddenly had to, she leaned down and gave him a hearty hug of her own before straightening again. ''After all the rain we've been having, digging should be easy,'' she told him. The ground was sure to be soaked under the thick layer of pine needles covering a good portion of it. Even Dry Creek held more water than she'd seen since last summer's storms.

"Okay if I look for some worms now?" Sam asked with a glance back at Adam.

"Sure," his father replied, his mouth curving. "Try not to get too grubby."

Promising nothing on that score, Sam grinned and was off and running toward the resort office and the storeroom that held a small shovel among its various supplies. By now, he was almost as familiar as she was with the place, Jane thought. And he was happier today than she'd ever seen him, that was clear.

Yes, something important had happened, all right. *I want my son back.* That was what Adam had told her weeks ago.

Now it very much seemed he'd gotten his wish. It was more than the fact that Sam would be with him beyond the summer. A lot more, Jane suspected. Their whole relationship, which had somehow been damaged, appeared to be back in good working order. She could only be pleased for both of them.

"Looks as though things have taken a turn for the better in the father and son department," she told Adam, closing the distance between them with determined steps. That wasn't what she'd planned on saying to him, but it served the purpose of breaking three days' worth of silence between them.

From his seat on the porch steps he only had to lift his gaze a short way to meet hers. "They have," he acknowledged, calmly enough, although his own eyes held the barest trace of moisture before he swiftly blinked it away. "He'll have another adjustment in store for him, of course, but I plan on doing everything I can to make it as easy as possible.''

Including a new house, Jane reflected. One that would put them both closer to Adam's parents after they left Glory Ridge behind them.

And they would be leaving it behind, of course. She'd never thought otherwise, not even after Adam had shared a night with her that she would never forget. She didn't, not for a minute, expect him to feel the same way. After all, he'd known women— probably a good many of them—who were down- right gorgeous. Women he'd shared nights with in the past.

And even if he did feel the same way, at least a little, it wouldn't change anything. She'd never been one to live in a fantasy world, so she didn't shirk meeting that truth head-on. Despite a physical joining that had put them as close as two people could get, there was no denying that fate had far different things in store for them.

Her future was here, in a spot she couldn't imagine leaving. He, on the other hand, had his life in Phoe- nix waiting for him—a life he'd apparently enjoyed having before coming to Glory Ridge. And now that life would include his son.

''I'm glad things worked out between you and Sam,'' she said, and meant it.

His gaze remained on hers. ''Thanks.''

She hooked her thumbs in her jean pockets. ''So your ex-wife's going to have two babies, huh?'' She tried hard for a casual tone and managed to achieve it.

''Uh-huh. Twins,'' he confirmed. ''Ariel's still ad- justing to the news. We discovered when Sam was born how much time and care one small baby demands. The prospect of two will take some getting used to, but she'll be fine.''

Both his words and the dry humor in his voice told Jane as plainly as if he'd said so that Adam wasn't carrying a torch for his ex-wife. Her remarriage hadn't broken his heart; that appeared clear.

It seemed he was free to enter into a serious relationship. Which didn't, of course, mean he was looking for one. And when he was, he'd no doubt set his sights on someone much like the woman he'd married—a woman he wouldn't find within miles of Glory Ridge. Even Harmony, for all its genuine friendliness, had no Boston blue-bloods among its residents.

''Haven't seen you for a while,'' he said, rousting Jane from her thoughts. The humor was gone, she noted. Beyond that, he wasn't giving her much clue to his feelings.

She attempted an offhand shrug. ''I've been busy keeping tabs on the construction crew and, uh, other things.''

''You've also been busy avoiding me,'' he didn't hesitate to remark.

Since there was no evading it, she settled for the simple truth. ''That, too.''

''I suppose I don't have to ask why.''

''I guess you don't,'' she confessed. ''And I suppose it's time to say I'm sorry for letting my temper take over.''

Which was all she'd offer on the subject, she vowed, even though she'd come to the conclusion that he'd had a point about her looking at herself through her father's eyes. Acknowledging even to herself that this man had no doubt been right hadn't been easy. In fact, she'd dragged her feet, still sporting ten painted toenails, every step of the way.

But the more she'd thought about it, the more Adam's theory made sense. One thing for sure, if regarding her image through other eyes had become an unconscious habit over the years, she'd be a lot better off breaking it and seeing herself for herself, no matter what she saw. That was what sheer common sense told her, and she had to agree.

"Apology accepted." Although Adam spoke matter of factly, the knowing glint in his eyes said that he'd picked up on at least some of what she hadn't admitted out loud. Maybe *everything* she hadn't admitted. When the slow smile that followed held a wealth of quiet satisfaction, she was sure of it.

She crossed her arms over the front of her checked shirt. "Don't put too much into that apology," she advised. "I'm not out to stroke your ego."

"Wouldn't think of it," he said blandly. *But I wouldn't mind having other parts of me stroked,* a suddenly smoky cast to his gaze added. *And stroking some of yours.*

So he still wanted her. Well, she still wanted him, too. Even ached for him, she had to concede.

The attraction between them was there. She'd given up any attempt to ignore it as a lost cause. They might be totally different people, but they could satisfy each other on one very basic level. That had been more than evident during an unforgettable night. At least he could satisfy her. Good grief, just remembering how he'd—

Adam's cell phone rang, halting her in mid-thought. He pulled the phone from his belt, never taking his eyes off her as he answered. "Lassiter here. Glad to hear from you," he said after a short pause. "Have you got anything for me?"

Jane watched a frown form on his wide and now tanned forehead as the mainly one-sided conversation continued. Whatever the subject, she had no trouble noting that it was serious enough for his frown to deepen to a dark slash before he issued some final words. "Thanks for checking it out. I owe you one."

"Bad news?" Jane ventured when he disconnected the call, her curiosity piqued.

"Interesting news," he told her. "I wouldn't say it's bad unless you decide to get fired up at me all over again for asking an acquaintance of mine to do a little background digging on your guest who likes to take hikes."

It was Jane's turn to frown. "Curt Bartlett?"

"Make that Curtis V. Bartlett." Adam paused. "Ever heard of CVB Development?"

She gave her head a quick shake.

"Neither have I," he admitted, "but my source tells me it's a firm based in Colorado that specializes in buying large tracts of land in the middle of nowhere as cheaply as possible. The head guy—that would be good ol' Curt—seems to favor a hands-on approach when it comes to picking likely targets to purchase."

Land in the middle of nowhere. That description would fit Glory Ridge, Jane knew. "And what do they do with the land once they have it?"

Adam's tone turned grim. "They bulldoze pretty much everything and put up vacation homes."

Jane's temper won out, but this time no part of it was directed at Adam. No, she was reserving her anger for the guest she'd gone out of her way to be nice to, the same seasoned outdoorsman who'd been going for more than hikes. Blast the man, he'd been scouting out *her* land as a prime candidate for a bulldozer!

"I'll show him hospitality," she snapped.

"You may have to wait. He could be communicating with nature right this minute," Adam pointed out dryly as he rose to his feet.

"Humph." She tossed a fleeting glance toward an early afternoon sky that already held a fair share of thick clouds. "If he is out, he'll be back once the wind picks up. He'll know another storm's on the way."

"Well, I'm sticking around, no matter how long it takes," Adam said. "You're not facing him alone."

There was enough steel underscoring that statement to stop any argument on Jane's part. Not that she wanted to argue. As far as she was concerned, they could both wait for the chance to deal with a scheming developer.

In fact, it wouldn't hurt at all, she decided, if they could put a short delay to good use and come up with a fitting goodbye before Curtis V. Bartlett was sent packing.

"THERE'S NO NEED to get riled," Curt told Jane in his characteristic drawl, looking down at her and offering a by now much-repeated phrase as his RV stood behind him pointed toward the highway, its well-tuned engine humming. "No need at all."

This time, his unsolicited advice had her baring her teeth. If she hadn't already planned a less physical revenge—one she dearly hoped would work out as intended—she knew she'd be in grave danger of launching a swift kick in his direction.

"You could do worse than selling the land to me," Curt continued in an oh-so-reasonable, let's-be-logical-here-folks tone, still doggedly pursuing his objective even after his guest status had been terminated. "This whole idea of turning the place into a honeymoon resort is a big gamble."

"I don't think so," Adam said, his voice low yet firm as he stood beside Jane in the parking lot.

Curt ignored that statement and kept his attention on Jane. "The money I can offer is a sure thing."

She curled her lip. "You can take your offer and stuff it." Rather than hiding her scorn, she made it plain as day. "There's no way I'd let this place be bulldozed by a sneaky outfit like yours. I don't deal with slime."

Finally, Curt's composure slipped. His expression, normally so affable, turned as dark as the building clouds overhead as he moved a step toward her.

Adam's abruptly sharp order halted him. "Stay where you are, Bartlett. If you don't, you'll be sorry, I promise."

The warning earned him a swift glare. "I can hold my own with you or any man, Lassiter."

"Could be," Adam said, a dangerous edge entering his voice. "We won't know until we put it to the test, will we?"

Jane ventured a glimpse at Adam's bright chrome wristwatch. It was fast approaching four o'clock. Perfect timing, she thought. At least, she hoped it was perfect. With the way the two men were trading hard stares, a fistfight could break out any minute.

Taut seconds passed before she looked behind her

and saw an animal barreling down the gravel path leading toward the parking lot. "Looks as though we're about to get company. I, uh, hope it's the kind we want."

Curt was more than tall enough to peer over her shoulder. "It's just Sweet Pea." He'd already been introduced to the resort's pet and had no fear of her.

Adam did a half turn. "If it is, she's moving a lot faster than she usually moves." He paused for a beat. "And doesn't she have a white stripe on her forehead, as well as down her back?"

"She does," Jane confirmed. She hesitated for a second. "I don't see any, though."

Curt frowned. "It has to be her."

"I don't think so," Adam contradicted slowly, suddenly going stock-still, as though rooted to the spot.

"Has to be," Curt repeated, although he didn't sound quite so certain anymore.

"I hope you're right," Jane whispered as the skunk ran straight toward them. "Unfortunately, I'm afraid you're not," she added when two beady eyes homed in on the trio.

"Damn," Adam muttered.

"Oh, dear," Jane got out with a gulp.

"Jeez, it's not her!" Curt's shout was still ringing in the air around them when he turned and ran toward his RV. The driver's door had scarcely shut behind him when he gunned the engine and drove off, spraying gravel as though a pack of hungry wolves was after him.

Dust was still settling back to earth when Jane retrieved the vanilla wafer she'd stuffed into a jeans pocket and crouched. "Good girl," she said, offering the wafer to the skunk.

"Seems you were right when you said she'd come running if she got a whiff of that," Adam told her with unruffled calm.

"Uh-huh." And she'd made sure Sweet Pea got a good whiff, Jane thought, before leaving her with Sam back at Pitt's Pride, and temporarily blocking the normal exit from her home under the porch with a piece of cardboard. "Vanilla wafers are her favorite. It's about the only thing she'll break a sweat to get to. I knew she'd track me down in a hurry once Sam let her out."

"Having someone around who favors wine over beer also came in handy, didn't it?"

"It did," she readily admitted. "I'll wash off the burned cork you gave me to hide the white stripe on her forehead later." Jane straightened and looked down the now-empty road. "I guess Curt was in a hurry," she said, her voice tinged with irony.

Once again standing beside her, Adam followed her gaze. "Can't figure out what was wrong with him," he remarked, matching her tone.

"Maybe he smelled something he didn't like."

She looked at Adam.

He looked at her.

They both burst out laughing at the same time. Before long they were roaring their heads off.

"Did it work?" Sam called as he came running up to them.

"Couldn't have worked better," Adam said.

Jane sputtered out a last laugh. "You did great," she told Sam. "Sweet Pea showed up at just the right time."

Sam gazed from one adult to the other. "Since I did so good," he said, "can we go fishing tomorrow?"

Jane cocked a brow. "Are you ready to get up early?"

Sam wasted no time in agreeing. "Sure."

She glanced at Adam. "How about you?"

At his short nod, Sam was all smiles for the second time that day. "Okay!"

"Not that I wouldn't rather sleep in," Adam offered for Jane's ears alone as his son bent to pet Sweet Pea. *With you,* his suddenly husky voice silently tacked on.

She wanted to sleep in, too. With him.

What she didn't want to do—couldn't afford to do, she knew full well—was forget that the future had far different things in store for them. Thankfully, any forgetfulness wouldn't be likely to happen with her attention fixed on being a fishing guide.

She'd just have to make sure her attention stayed fixed there, Jane told herself, no matter how downright devastating one particular guest looked as he once again attempted to outsmart a clever trout.

Chapter Eleven

He'd give the worm stealer a run for his money.

Flat on his back in his solitary bed, Adam laced his hands behind his head as his wake-up call in the form of a classic rock tune played in the background. At the very least, he'd make a fat fish work for those worms, he vowed. He wasn't just letting them be nibbled off the hook. Not today.

"And now for our local forecast," the radio announcer said when the tune faded away. "The good news is that the unusually powerful weather pattern is shifting to a more moderate cycle that will still give us some occasional rain, but not the steady downpours we've been experiencing. The bad news is that one last doozy of a storm, maybe the biggest yet this year, could hit the higher elevations a few hundred miles to the north tonight, and there's no telling at this point whether it will drift down toward Harmony if that happens. So batten the hatches, folks, just in case."

A break in the nightly rains sounded good, Adam thought. Even without that puzzling dream to disturb his sleep in the past twenty-four hours, and a patched roof that didn't leak over his head, noisy bouts of on-and-off thunder combined with steadily howling winds hardly promised a restful night.

Unless you were an eight-year-old boy, he amended, hauling himself out of bed with a groan. Sam could sleep through almost anything.

Sure enough, his son looked bright-eyed and well-rested when they joined Jane after a quick breakfast and headed down to the lake, their fishing gear in hand. Although the rain had stopped, water rushed through Dry Creek as they crossed the narrow bridge.

"Wow, it's pretty high," Sam said, looking past the short railing. "Do you think it's gonna spill over?" he asked Jane.

"It hasn't in all the years I've been here," she assured him. "It happened once a long time ago, but from what I've been told, it wasn't enough to do much damage."

Adam studied the water. It looked high to him, too. "Have you ever had as many big storms this close together while you've been here?"

She reached up to tug down the bill of her baseball cap. "Maybe not quite this close together," she acknowledged with a small shrug. "Fortunately, the storm pattern's supposed to change."

So she'd heard the same forecast he had, he reflected to himself. And she didn't seem too worried, despite the possibility of more rain tonight. Since she knew the area a lot better than he did, he decided to take that as a good sign.

The sun was just coming up as Adam rowed toward the middle of the lake. He thought about the rickety dock that would soon get a much-needed face-lift and the old wooden boats destined to be refinished and put back in good shape before Glory Ridge Honeymoon Haven opened its doors.

Once all the cabins had an outside coat of fresh paint, the interiors would get a newer, brighter look—still rustic, but with several more creature comforts than they currently had. Small microwaves, electric coffeemakers, some new furniture—including new beds—and mattresses. Everything would be in place to welcome the first honeymooners. And if they had reserved one of the "deluxe" two-bedroom models, a newly installed hot tub in the second bedroom, complete with a stack of thick, fluffy towels, would top off the amenities.

The resort office was scheduled for a makeover, as well. It would feature the full-size computer Adam had ordered, scheduled for shipment next week. Teaching Jane how to operate it was a top priority. Once he was gone, she'd be on her own there.

As if he, too, were considering a time when he'd no longer be at Glory Ridge, gliding over the deep blue waters of Quail Lake, Sam watched the sunrise with his chin propped in his hands and a wistful expression on his face. "I wish we didn't hafta leave here," he told Jane, who sat beside him rummaging in the tackle box, "but Dad says we gotta."

She paused in her task, her fingers stilling on a colorfully striped bobber. "It's probably for the best when you think about it," she said after a moment, her voice soft in the quiet all around them. "Once you're back in school, you'll make new friends in no time. Plus you'll have a new house to live in," she reminded him. "I'd say that all adds up to a lot to look forward to."

Sam nodded slowly, as though reluctantly agreeing

with the wisdom of those words. "I'm gonna find the biggest worm I got so I can catch the biggest fish."

"Good plan," she said in an upbeat tone. When he bent to forage for bait in the coffee can he'd filled, Jane's gaze locked with Adam's.

She knew, he thought, watching her hazel eyes calmly stare back at him. Beyond knowing that he'd be leaving as originally scheduled, she knew why. Knew that this was still a foreign place to him, as much as the life he'd led before coming here would be foreign to her. And she accepted it. He was all but positive of that.

What she didn't know was that it would be hard to leave her. How hard, he hadn't realized himself until this minute. Logic told him that beginning a physical relationship that could only be headed no-where had probably been a mistake. But something gut-deep inside him contended otherwise.

You feel too good when you're with her, it said. *Far from the prickly female you first thought her to be, she has a warmth that draws you in once you get past her defenses. Just hope she lets you back into her bed as soon as the opportunity arises.*

Wise or not, Adam realized he was going with his gut.

Another long moment passed before Jane pulled her gaze away. While Adam continued to row, she bent her head and went back to her task, telling her-self that it was time—past time—to resume her guide role. Trading stares with a man who had developed a talent for seeing straight inside her wasn't the best way to keep her thoughts where they should be. After all, she was here to help his son land a trout worth keeping.

And in the next few hours she did exactly that. While morning headed toward midday and birds chattered in the tall trees circling the lake, Sam reeled in another keeper and wound up looking fully pleased with his achievement.

Meanwhile, Adam had come up empty. Again.

"Sure you don't want me to give you some pointers?" she said out of the corner of her mouth, keeping her voice low enough to make that question private between them.

"Not a chance," he muttered in reply. "I'm out to get the better of a wily, worm-stealing fish today, and it's a personal mission."

Just then, something launched itself out of the water behind them and landed with a large splash, as if to say, *Don't bet on being successful, pal.*

Jane struggled to hold back a laugh and almost succeeded. Almost, but not quite. A muffled snort still managed to escape her.

Adam growled out what seemed to be a cuss and stuck with the task. Bending forward, he narrowed his eyes on his bobber, searching for the slightest signal that something was toying with his line.

He was persistent. Jane had to give him that. Also stubborn. Leaving him to it, she studied the lake, noting how the water had risen after the recent storms. It was as high as she'd ever seen it—just like the water rushing through Dry Creek.

She frowned. Although she'd done her best not to show it earlier that morning with Sam so enthusiastic about another round of fishing, she couldn't help but be concerned, at least a little. Then again, Glory

Ridge had withstood everything Mother Nature had sent its way in the past. That reflection eased her mind.

"I've got something," Adam suddenly said, regaining her attention in a flash. "Something big." The way his line bowed, tight with tension, indicated he was right.

Jane was afraid that he would try to reel in his catch too soon, instead of playing it out until the fish tired. She soon learned, however, that Adam had listened to what she'd told Sam. He let his patience rule, slowly and surely bringing his catch in, until Jane was able to bend over and scoop the fish up in the net. She soon realized she'd need to use both hands and some muscle to accomplish that task, because Adam had indeed reeled in a fat—and unmistakably familiar—trout.

"Wow, Dad, did you catch Clever Clyde?" Sam asked as Jane set the wiggling fish, net and all, in the bottom of the boat.

Adam stared down at his nemesis. "By God, I think I have."

"You did," Jane assured him. The trout continued to thrash in the net, and despite her practical nature, Jane felt a small pang of sympathy at seeing a legend finally caught. She knew the seasoned fishermen Clever Clyde had outsmarted wouldn't share her feelings. They'd probably be cheering, and she'd hardly be surprised if Adam raised a cheer of his own. In fact, she waited for one to come, but it was Sam who finally broke the silence.

"Are you gonna eat him, Dad?"

Adam studied his still-struggling catch for a long moment, then slowly shook his head. "No."

So, he'd decided to mount it, Jane thought with disappointment. She'd always considered eating anything caught by the rules a fair outcome of a fishing expedition. Stuffing an animal for a trophy, though, was another matter.

Her forehead knitted as Adam crouched and removed the hook from the trout's mouth, taking longer than an expert but getting the job done. He picked up the wiggling fish and tossed it back into the water.

"You let Clever Clyde go," Sam said, wonder in his voice, as though he couldn't believe it.

"I caught it," Adam told his son. "I know it and so does that worm stealer. And that's what counts." A wry smile curved his mouth. "Besides, he was probably too tough to eat."

"What do you think, Jane?" Sam asked. "Was Clever Clyde too tough to eat?"

"Could be," she replied after a moment, finally finding her voice. A part of her was still a little stunned that Adam had tossed the fish that had plagued him for weeks back into the lake, offering the wily trout a second chance at life. But what stunned her more—far more—was her reaction.

Because she had reacted. Swiftly and unmistakably. Her heart was telling her so in no uncertain terms, and she knew that for all she'd sworn she would never do it, it had happened.

Just like that, in a matter of instants, she'd fallen hook, line and sinker for a fancy man.

JANE WAS STILL coming to terms with that undeniable truth as they docked and started up the path to the cabins. Reeled in, netted and hauled aboard without so much as a struggle—that was what she'd been. And all by a rookie fisherman who was turning out to be far more than she'd first expected.

Yes, he'd landed her—and the heart she'd guarded for years—good and proper. And she had no idea what to do about it.

Deciding to concentrate on something else—anything else, for the moment—she again studied the water as they crossed the bridge over Dry Creek. It hadn't gone down, she noted. But it hadn't gone up, either. And, although it was past noon, there wasn't so much as a wisp of a cloud in the sky. She chose to take that as a promising sign.

They met Travis after the bridge was behind them. Decked out in his usual battered jeans and a T-shirt, he braked to a quick halt on his bicycle and greeted the group with a wave.

"Want to come over to my place?" he asked Sam. "My dad's got some time to help us work on the tree house before it gets dark."

Sam turned to his father for permission, clearly ready, willing and eager to take Travis up on that invitation. Then his eyes lit up several watts as Travis added, "We're having grilled burgers for dinner. My mom said before she left for work that you could spend the night again, if you want to."

"I want to," Sam said at once. "Can I, Dad?"

Adam mulled the invitation over. "You'll behave, do as you're told and be a good guest?"

"Yep."

"Okay."

Sam and Travis smacked palms in a high five.

"Since we haven't had lunch yet," Adam continued, "I'll fix you boys a sandwich and then drive you over. We can put your bicycle in the trunk,'' he told Travis. He glanced down at the small cooler he held. ''Think your parents would like to grill the trout Sam just caught?''

''Yeah, they like fish.'' Travis screwed his face into a grimace. ''I don't.''

''Then I'll put the cooler in the car,'' Adam said. ''While I do that, why don't you get washed up and we'll have lunch.''

The boys soon headed off to the Lassiters' cabin, Travis pedaling slowly and Sam running along. Adam looked at Jane. ''How about if I come over to your place and make you dinner tonight?''

He was talking about more than dinner. She knew it by the gleam that had sparked to life in his eyes. She also knew declining would be safer. If she didn't, she'd risk letting him see that back on the boat things had changed in a heartbeat.

Changed for her, that is. Because nothing else about the situation had changed. She was staying. He was going.

But he wasn't going yet, and she suddenly found herself unable to turn down the chance to spend another night—another long and sure-to-be-memorable night—with him.

''All right,'' she said at last, then quickly added, ''I have some things to do back at my cabin this afternoon.'' For all that she couldn't turn him down, she needed some time to herself right now. ''See you around six?''

He lowered his head and dropped a brief kiss on her mouth. ''I'll be there,'' he murmured against her lips. Far from a casual comment, it was an intimate promise that sent a quiver of anticipation sliding down her spine.

"Yeah, well, what's for dinner, now that you've given the fish away?" she asked, summoning the lightest tone she could muster.

He straightened, and for the first time she got the full impact of a wide, somewhat wicked and very male grin that threatened to charm her right off her booted feet. "I'll come up with something to keep up our strength."

"Oh." That was all she could manage to get out, so she started moving again, in a near march this time, and they soon parted ways. She made for the office, where she returned the tackle box and other equipment to the supply room and checked the answering machine. She found a message and placed a call that had her booking her first reservation for a honeymoon couple who'd be arriving in November.

"We'd planned on going to a larger resort," the bride-to-be told her, "but when we saw the brochure my mother picked up, we decided that Glory Ridge would be cozier."

"I'm sure you'll enjoy your stay," Jane said in her best courteous hostess manner. She might have to put up with the sight of newlyweds wrapped around each other, she thought, but at least none of them would be a sneaky developer.

Once the call was completed, she dutifully wrote the information in her ledger book. Then she headed for Pitt's Pride. Back in her cabin, she tossed her ball cap on a hook by the door, walked to the bathroom and washed her hands. As she looked into the mirror where she'd studied her reflection days earlier,

Adam's advice to stop see herself through her father's eyes once again rang in her mind.

Until that changes, you may never be the person you can be. That was what he'd said. But what he'd really meant, she recognized with sudden insight, was that she might never be the *woman* she could be.

With each passing year as she'd grown older, she'd become more and more confident in her abilities and content with herself as a person. The female part of growing up, however, had proved to be difficult, right from the time she'd hit puberty.

But it didn't have to be that way.

She could be a woman clear down to her toes.

Starting tonight...if she had the nerve.

"Of course you have the nerve," Jane assured the image that stared back at her. "You're no wimp."

And if she had the nerve, Ellen had given her everything else she'd need.

Nibbling on her lower lip, Jane debated the matter for a long moment. Then, her choice made, she started for the bedroom, thinking that if Adam could bowl her over with a grin, well, she could do her best to make an impact, too. Maybe she couldn't bowl him over, but she could give it a try.

The one thing she wouldn't—couldn't—do was let him know that nothing in her private and personal world would be quite the same after today. She may have lost her heart, she thought, but she still had her pride.

ADAM DECIDED on beef stir-fry for dinner, since he had all the makings. Besides being one of his efforts that had won him praise in the past, most of the work was in the preparation, which he could do before heading over to Jane's. Then once he got there, getting a meal on the table would be a snap and he could get on to other things.

He damn well wanted to get on to other things.

That plan in mind, he arrived at Pitt's Pride promptly at six, holding a bag containing the sliced meat and vegetables, together with the rice he'd already steamed. In the other hand, he gripped a bottle of the slightly chilled, fruity red wine he'd opted for. A gentle breeze ruffled his hair as he took the two steps up to the front porch. No blustery winds today, he noted, and only a thin cloud covering overhead. Nothing, thankfully, to indicate an approaching storm.

He knocked on the screen door and was surprised when Jane soon appeared in the same outfit she'd worn for the business fair. She held the door open and let it shut behind him with a soft snap.

"I didn't realize we were dressing for dinner," he said.

He'd showered and shaved before coming, but had only donned a pair of Levi's and a black denim shirt similar to what he'd worn that morning. In contrast, his hostess had done a total turnabout, complete with a light application of makeup that again had her eyes looking bigger, her cheeks sporting a healthy glow and her lips moist with the same shade of creamy pink that tinted her short, oval-shaped nails.

She also smelled like heaven. Or maybe sin would be a better description. And that was completely new.

"I decided this outfit might as well be put to some use—plus I have something to celebrate," she told him, and went on to explain that she'd taken the first reservation for Glory Ridge Honeymoon Haven that afternoon. She aimed a sweeping glance over him. "You look fine as you are."

But she looked a lot better than fine, he thought, taking another whiff of her. "What's that perfume you're wearing?"

"Oh, just something Ellen gave me for my birthday," she informed him in an offhand tone.

He cocked a brow. "The one coming up in October?"

"Mmm-hmm."

He'd by no means forgotten her sister's generosity. In fact, he planned on dipping into that honey jar tonight for the protection she'd provided. He also recalled that Jane had hedged about revealing the rest of the gift. He'd never suspected it would turn out to be a small bottle of floral-laced dynamite that threatened to knock a man on his butt.

"Did she give you anything else?" he had to ask.

"One more thing," Jane said. And that was all she said.

He frowned down at her. "You're going to let me drive myself crazy wondering about it, aren't you?"

She smiled. "I'll show it to you later."

Later suddenly seemed way too vague—for him and the avid male curiosity she was managing to rouse right along with the rest of him. "After dinner?" he prompted.

She hesitated for a moment, her smile slipping a little. Then she nodded her agreement, and it was his turn to smile as he took swift steps toward the small kitchen. "Won't take me long to get a meal on the table."

And it didn't. Just over an hour later they were

finishing the cleanup. "I have to admire your efficiency," Jane told him as she rinsed the last dish.

He moved up behind her and bent to nibble on her neck. "It helps to have an incentive."

She slanted her head to give him better access. "Mmm. I guess it does."

"Do I see the rest of that present now?" he whispered in her ear.

She dragged in what sounded like a steadying breath, as though gearing herself up for a major effort. "You can have another glass of wine while I, uh, get ready to show it to you."

"Don't be long." It came out as more of an order than a request, despite him doing his damnedest to be patient when he really wanted to swing Jane up in his arms and carry her off to bed. Now.

Without promising one way or the other how speedy she'd be, Jane left him to head for the bedroom. At least she was going in the right direction, he thought, looking after her.

He refilled a small juice glass with wine, ignoring the indignity the premium vintage was suffering, and settled himself in the faded, russet, overstuffed chair. He considered building a fire in the small fireplace, decided that would take too long and just sat back to wait. And wait.

He thought about shouting "Hallelujah!" when he heard the bedroom door open, but Jane spoke first as he set his glass down on the narrow pine end table at his elbow.

"You have to shut your eyes," she called, her voice drifting through the bedroom doorway.

He resisted the urge to sigh at another delay.

"They're closed," he called back, suiting action to word.

She approached so quietly that he never heard her coming. Only the smell of that killer perfume teasing his nose and tempting lower parts of him told him she was near before she set her small hand in his and urged him to his feet with a light tug.

"Just keep those eyes shut until we get to the bedroom and I say the okay," she warned as she led him across the room.

"This had better be good," he grumbled half-heartedly. But he played fair and didn't even peek until she dropped his hand and gave the go-ahead.

"Okay, you can open them."

He opened them. And then he stared.

"Is it…good enough?" she asked after a hushed moment.

He barely heard her. He was too busy letting his eyes look their fill, taking in every inch of a slender body clad in what could probably be called a night-gown. If he thought the perfume was a killer, this short, gauzy, snowy-white confection, ruffled at neck and hem but nearly transparent everywhere else, was positively lethal.

"Good enough?" he somehow managed to mutter. "You have got to be kidding."

But she wasn't.

He discovered that after finally rousing himself enough to raise his gaze to her face. The wary look in her eyes, the uneasy flick of her tongue across her lips, the way she held herself still—everything silently told him that she'd been dead serious.

He took a swift step forward and wrapped his arms around her. "Good doesn't begin to cover it," he said. "You're on your way to driving me right up the wall."

"Really?"

"You'd better believe it." The words were firm enough, he was glad to note, even though they came out sounding a little breathless. Giving up on speech for the moment, he lowered his mouth to hers and kissed her. He had to marvel all over again at how sweet she tasted, and how one long and lingering bite could make him lose his control. He'd kissed his first girl many years ago, but not even that episode had managed to rattle him as badly.

Now, as a full-grown man, he wanted more than kisses, of course. And wanting was rapidly becoming needing, he recognized, feeling everything inside him clench with the impact of that realization, as though he'd taken a fist to the gut.

The wanting was familiar by now; he'd been experiencing it for days—maybe weeks, if he were honest with himself. But the needing was new. And potent.

He needed to make love with Jane. Preferably sometime in the next ten seconds.

Breaking the kiss, he stared down at her, pleased to note that her breathing had become nearly as ragged as his. "Don't move," he told her. Releasing his grip on her, he made fast tracks toward the dresser. There, he set down the cell phone hooked to his belt and reached into the honey jar. A smile of pure—or maybe anything but pure, he decided—satisfaction curved his mouth as he pulled out a foil packet.

He started shedding his clothes on his way back to the bed and completed the job in short order. Jane watched his every move. And he watched her. In fact, he couldn't look away.

"How about if you keep that nightgown on for a while?" he suggested, taking her into his arms once more.

The barest hint of a twinkle lit her gaze as she stared up at him. "You really like it, don't you?"

"Oh, yeah," he replied with feeling. Picking her right up off her bare feet, he swung her around in a fast circle just for the hell of it and laid her on the bed.

She glanced at the tall brass floor lamp providing the only light in the room. "Doesn't seem the electricity's going out tonight," she said as he stretched out next to her.

"I don't think so." And he could only be damn glad that all remained quiet outside. "I'm not switching off that lamp anytime soon, either," he promptly informed her as he ran a hand over the short gauzy white gown that hid nothing from his sight. Unable to resist, he dipped his head to take a small, pink-tipped breast into his mouth right through the fabric.

And, although he lingered briefly, purposefully, he didn't stop there, spurred on by the murmurs his questing mouth and seeking hands were creating. He held back as long as he could, until the need building in him could no longer be denied. Then he applied protection and joined his body with hers.

"You feel good." He had to clear his throat to get the words out as he propped his weight on his elbows and found the familiar rhythm. "No, scratch that. You feel great."

Jane wrapped her arms around Adam's neck, thinking he was the one who felt great. Not that she doubted for a moment that he'd meant that last, roughly murmured statement. She was giving him pleasure even as she received it.

And seeing her wearing something she'd had to stiffen every bit of her resolve to put on had given him pleasure, too. Again she had no doubts on that score. Not now.

Somewhere during the last few minutes, she'd discovered that being a woman clear to her toes could be a wondrous thing. And holding the power to drive a man right up the wall, as Adam had phrased it, was downright amazing. At least it was to her.

She would never forget how it had built her confidence—how *he* had built her confidence. Long after their time together was over, she would remember.

And she would smile, she told herself, despite the fact that a piece of her heart would go with him.

Jane sighed. No, she wouldn't forget, and she wouldn't regret for one second what they'd shared. Instead, despite being a long way from the most beautiful creature ever to grace the planet, she would make the most of the hand Mother Nature had dealt her and do her best to be the confident woman she could be—on the outside and, even more important, on the inside—years after Adam was gone.

Not that she was letting him go right this minute. Not hardly, she thought, feeling that heady sense of female power roll through her to send the blood zinging in her veins. The night was still young and she had plans for this male.

The element of surprise was in her favor when she gave his strong shoulders a firm push and rolled them both over to reverse positions. In a flash, she was staring down at the man stretched out under her.

"You could have told me you wanted to be on top," he said, his voice more than deep and husky enough to bluntly display his desire.

She brushed her fingers through his crisp chest hair. "I decided showing was better than telling."

"Hmm." He ran his warm palms up her thighs until they reached the ruffled hem of her bunched-up nightgown. "Not that I'm complaining with the recent, uh, turns of events, but I feel obliged to point out that this doesn't work unless we keep moving."

"I know," she said, her lips curving. "I plan on moving, believe me." And she did. In fact, she wasted no time in setting an increasingly rapid pace.

"Why am I thinking you're enjoying being in charge?" he asked.

"Because I am."

She might have followed that short, undeniably true, statement with a wry laugh, but suddenly, her body asserted itself, urging her onward, and all traces of humor fled. Before long she was poised on the brink. And then she went over with a quiet cry.

"Yes!" Adam gritted as she slid down, boneless now, to rest her head on his shoulder. In the next instant, he shuddered under her.

"So good," she heard him mutter. "So damn good."

Then silence reigned, broken only by the sound of their mingled breaths. Soon his breathing slowed and turned even enough to tell her he was on the verge of sleep.

Minutes passed without so much as a move on his part before she snuggled her nose into the crook of his neck and said words she would never have said if she hadn't been sure only she could hear them.

"I love you," she whispered.

Then she took in the comforting scent of pine soap and pure male and waited for her slumbering lover to gather his resources. Something told her that neither of them would be getting much rest that night...and that suited her just fine.

Chapter Twelve

A shrill ring jarred Adam out of a sound sleep. It took him a minute to realize the sound came from the cell phone he'd left on Jane's dresser and another moment to haul himself out of bed. The bedroom was dark enough to have him stumbling across the room. His first thought was that it might be Sam calling for some reason. He couldn't imagine that any of his clients or other business acquaintances would be trying to reach him at this ungodly early hour.

"Lassiter here," he answered, sounding groggy even to his ears.

"Thank goodness I got through to somebody at Glory Ridge," a deep voice said.

Something was familiar about that voice, but his brain still felt partly on hold. "Who is this?"

"Tom Kennedy."

The police chief? Adam woke up in a hurry, but before he could get a word out, Tom went on.

"I've been trying to call the resort office phone, but all I got was the answering machine. I finally tracked your cousin down at his hotel on the west coast and got your cell phone number."

Adam frowned. "You called Ross?"

"Yep."

Adam knew the Haywards weren't due back from their vacation until the end of the week. The news that Tom had gone to the trouble of reaching Ross had his mind leaping to a conclusion he didn't want to consider but had to. "Is Sam all right?"

That question brought Tom up short. "Your son? Isn't he with you?"

"No, he spent the night at the Malloy place."

"Then I'm sure he's fine," Tom said. "I wanted to make certain you folks at Glory Ridge were okay."

Adam raked a hand through his sleep-mussed hair. He knew he was missing something, he just didn't know what. "Why wouldn't we be okay?"

Tom blew out a breath. "Land sakes, isn't it raining up there?"

Before Adam could reply, a hard—and undeniably familiar—pounding started on the cabin roof. "I guess it is," he admitted. "I didn't hear anything until now."

"It's been pouring on and off for hours in town," Tom said. "Mostly on. The weatherman says the rain's bound to be even worse in the mountains."

Adam walked to the single bedroom window, bare of any curtains, and glanced out at what resembled a wall of water more than anything else. "It's coming down hard," he confirmed. "I can make out that much, although the sun hasn't come up yet."

"The sun's been up for quite a while," Tom told him. "It's close to nine o'clock."

Now it was Adam's turn to be brought up short. A glance down at the luminous dial on his watch, which was all he wore at the moment, proved the police chief correct, however. "It's pitch-dark out here."

"Damn. That's what I was afraid of," Tom said. "The reason I've been trying to reach somebody up there is to find out about any signs of flooding, because this rain isn't letting up anytime soon, according to the weather service. See if you can track Jane Pitt down and ask her to call me back."

Adam turned toward the bed and saw that the woman he'd made love with again and again through the night, until they'd both fallen into an exhausted sleep, was sitting up against the pillows with the bedspread tucked under her arms. "I don't have to track her down," he said. "She's with me."

Tom hesitated for a scarce second, just long enough to indicate that news had taken him by surprise. "Better let me talk to her."

"Right." Adam walked over and handed the phone to Jane. "It's Tom Kennedy."

She glanced at the window, as though she'd guessed the weather was the reason for the chief's call, then spoke into the phone. "Yes, Tom."

Adam retrieved his cotton briefs, denim shirt and Levi's from where they'd landed on the floor in his earlier haste. He'd taken better care of Jane's nightgown when he'd finally tugged it off her. Now it rested at the very bottom of the bed in all its near-transparent glory, he noted as he dressed and sat on the edge of the mattress to pull on his boots.

Jane disconnected the call and handed the phone back to him. "I have to check things out. Everything is probably all right, but…"

"But the creek, given the way it winds right through the middle of the resort, could be a problem,'' Adam finished at her hesitation. Even though the creek had apparently never posed much of a problem before, he figured it needed to be said.

"There's always a possibility,'' she allowed.

He hooked the phone on his belt, slapped his hands on his knees and got to his feet. "Then let's check things out.''

"You don't have to—''

"I'm going with you,'' he said firmly. The last thing he wanted to do was argue the point. He just wanted the job done. "I'll hit the bathroom while you get dressed.''

She sighed in resignation. "Even Sweet Pea has the smarts to stay under cover until it stops raining, but okay, let's both get soaked.''

He looked down at her. "If it turns out there is no problem, we can come back here and get out of our wet clothes soon enough.'' He paused, his lips curving. "And you can put that sexy excuse for a nightgown back on.''

She smiled. "Maybe,'' she said.

"Definitely,'' he countered. And then he made fast tracks for the bathroom while he had the last word.

In the end, Jane came up with rain slickers for both of them, hers several sizes smaller than the one she gave him. "Good thing Aunt Maude was a fairly big woman or that wouldn't fit you,'' she told him as they left Pitt's Pride. Her tone was upbeat in spite of the darkly ominous sky and the thick sheets of rain that continued to pour down, soaking everything in sight.

They slogged their way down the narrow gravel path and soon met the slightly wider one leading to the lake. Adam soon heard the sound of rushing water. Despite the downpour, his ears could make it out clearly.

Seconds later, what his eyes saw brought him to a dead halt.

Rather than merely rushing through the creek, the swiftly moving water had overflowed its rocky, winding banks several feet on each side. Even as he watched, it crept inches closer to where he stood.

"Hell," he bit out, recalling how he'd once been stranded on a business trip when a peaceful river had turned into a raging torrent that had wiped out everything within a hundred-mile radius.

This was no river, of course, although it resembled a small one at the moment. But then, the creek didn't have to overflow its banks by even a half mile on each side to put the whole resort under water. Cabins that had stood for who knows how long might be washed clear away, replaced by no more than a thick layer of mud.

That was a worst-case scenario, true. But it could happen. The grim possibility had to be faced, Adam knew.

"Oh, my God," Jane whispered from where she stood at his side. The sheer shock on her face combined with the quiet apprehension in her voice indicated that she'd come to the same conclusion.

Adam reached under his slicker and took out his phone. Seconds later he was talking to Harmony's veteran police chief. "Tom," he said without any preliminaries, watching the steadily rising water, "I think we have a major problem here."

THE NEXT HOUR PASSED QUICKLY. After Adam's call to the police chief, Jane phoned the construction crew she'd been dealing with, since they hadn't, to no surprise, shown up for work as usual that morning. "We were waiting to see if you wanted us to come out in spite of what's looking more and more like one devil of a rainstorm," the foreman told her. When she explained the situation, he wasted no time in offering help. Two truckloads of sandbags, together with the crew plus some of their co-workers, arrived in short order.

As the nonstop rain continued, Jane was recognizing that the only chance to save the resort from turning into little more than a muddy wasteland was to build a makeshift wall on both sides of the creek. Then it would be time to hope and pray the stacked sandbags held until the storm feeding the already full creek blew through and the water began to recede.

"We just may see the sun before it sets tonight," Tom Kennedy told her when he arrived on the heels of the construction people. "That's the latest forecast, anyway. And then it looks as though this danged stubborn weather pattern will finally change for the better."

But the sober expression that settled on his face as he got his first glimpse of the overflowing creek said that change might not come soon enough.

She realized it, as well, but she was still hoping, and praying, anyway.

"More help's coming," he told her, tugging his wide-brimmed hat lower on his forehead when a sudden gust of wind threatened to blow it off.

And more help came, until it seemed as though half of Harmony was there. Jane knew Adam had called the Malloys to explain what was going on, so she wasn't surprised to see her sister and brother-in-law arriving with Travis and Sam. Like many of the people hefting sandbags, the foursome wore rain slickers. Sam's was too big for him. The garment reached almost to the ground, and its long vinyl sleeves were rolled up several times so his small hands could stick out.

"I canceled my appointments," Ellen said. "Nobody needs to get her hair done in this weather, anyway."

Jane did her best to summon a smile and concluded that her effort fell short when her sister frowned in concern. "What can I do to help?" Ellen asked.

Jane didn't have to point out that neither of them could heft the industrial-size sandbags. The fact was, she'd given it a try after the first truckload arrived, only to receive a steely look from Adam as he'd grabbed it from her, one that promised retribution if she tried it again.

"Folks around here could probably use some hot coffee," Mitch Malloy said in his typically easygoing fashion. "The weather's not cold, but it sure the heck is wet." And with those bluntly true words, he turned and left the group.

Probably headed for a sandbag he could throw over his broad shoulder and haul around, Jane thought glumly, gazing after the sole rancher left in her family. Despite her recent discovery of the benefits of "woman power," right now she had to wish she were a man so she could put her back to good use.

"My loving husband is right," Ellen said. "I've got coffee detail."

Jane nodded. "Better use the electric coffeemaker

in the office. It'll be easier.'' She didn't have to add that the coffeemaker in question was older than the hills. Ellen was no stranger to Glory Ridge.

As though seconding that thought, Ellen rolled her eyes. ''Let's hope it holds out.''

''We got some cookies at our cabin,'' Sam said. ''Double fudge, 'cause those are my favorite. I could go get them.''

''The cabin may be locked,'' Jane told him. In fact, she was pretty sure it was, since Adam hadn't returned there that morning.

''I can get the key from my dad. I saw him in the parking lot when we pulled in. He was talking to one of the men from the construction company about getting more sandbags. I asked if I could help, but they said I was too little.''

''Well, you can help now.'' Ellen took charge on the domestic front. ''You guys go for the cookies and meet me at the office. We'll set something up there.''

The boys were off and running when Ellen looked at Jane, rain dripping off the hood of her bright yellow slicker. ''Are you all right?''

''Sure.'' She wasn't about to say that her worries were multiplying like rabbits as time passed and the storm showed no signs of easing one blasted bit. That wouldn't serve any purpose but worrying her sister.

Ellen studied her for a long moment. ''I'll have the coffee done soon. Make sure you have a cup.''

''I will if I want some later,'' Jane hedged. Her stomach was flat empty, something she acknowledged to herself as Ellen departed, but she couldn't spare a thought for food. All she could think about was Glory Ridge's fate. All she could do was watch to see if the makeshift wall held.

And hope. And pray.

Yards away, Adam passed her, hefting another sandbag. It wasn't the worry but the lack of any expression at all on Jane's face that had him setting his burden down and making a quick detour. She needed something to do, he recognized.

He had to admit to being glad he had plenty to keep himself busy, even though working in a driving rain was no picnic. At least the job kept his mind from wandering to a newly surfaced memory of whispered words he'd either heard on the verge of sleep or dreamed after tumbling over.

I love you.

Had the words come from Jane's lips, or were they a product of his imagination?

He wished to hell he knew, because the memory was nagging at him like a sore tooth. He couldn't deny that even as he blocked the question for which he had no answer out one more time. Once again he reminded himself that he had plenty to do, along with the rest of the men scurrying around him. And whatever Jane had or hadn't said the night before, her attention was focused exactly where he'd expect it to be right now. He knew what Glory Ridge meant to her.

"You look waterlogged," he told her, attempting as wry a tone as he could produce, when he really wanted to reach out and tug her into his arms.

"So do you," she countered, matching his tone as she gave him a sweeping once-over. "A person could drown in the puddle you're standing there making, and those boots will never be the same, Slick.''

Ah, so she still had spunk. He was relieved to see it. ''I think the troops in the trenches could use some moral support,'' he said, nodding toward where men were stacking sandbags in a race against time that nevertheless somehow managed to be organized. ''I know I could.''

''All right,'' she said after a moment. ''I'm going crazy just watching.''

He flashed her a smile. ''Figured you were.''

She followed him to where he'd left the sandbag and they both joined the mix of Harmony residents who hadn't hesitated to offer a helping hand. Across the creek, the construction crew, aided by other volunteers, erected a twin wall. Jane waved at them.

''You're doing a great job,'' she called.

Hopefully, all their efforts would prove to be enough, Adam thought as he stacked his bag in the next open spot and went back for another load. By the time he'd returned, however, water was lapping near the top of the wall and another layer had to be added.

And so it went. More sandbags arriving by the truckload. Another rise in the swiftly rushing water. Jane cheering the workers on.

And the fierce storm raging around them, slowly and surely helping the water have its way, inch by inch. Finally, the narrow bridge across the creek became its victim, all traces of a structure that had probably stood since the birth of the resort washed away. Just like that, it was gone.

''Can't stack these sandbags much higher,'' Tom

said grimly, stopping beside Adam for a moment. "Things look bad."

He couldn't deny it. But damned if he'd say it, not after seeing Jane watch that old bridge turn to little more than chunks of weathered wood in an instant and noting her flinch as if she'd suffered a blow.

He wasn't admitting defeat. By God, he wasn't!

"We can beat this," he said, instead, gritting out the words as he fisted his hands at his sides. "This storm has to stop sometime."

Thunder crashed overhead as if to mock him. Somehow, it only strengthened his resolve.

In the hours that followed, people came and went in staggered shifts, getting coffee, taking short breaks from the relentless rain.

Adam stayed. And so did Jane.

At first he put the sight down to sheer wishful thinking when the thick layer of dark clouds overhead showed signs of breaking up at last. But then Adam caught the barest patch of clear blue just as the water was once again threatening to overflow its bounds. Long, tense minutes passed, and still the rain poured down.

"We can beat this," he said yet again, repeating the words to himself like a litany as the rain gradually slackened. Before too much time had passed, the winds died down and only a drizzle fell. Finally, the rain stopped completely.

The real question, however, was how the flood waters would respond. Adam shrugged out of his slicker and narrowed his eyes in concentration as he searched for the slightest sign that nature had given up the battle to wreak havoc. When he found it, saw the slow but seemingly steady drop in the swiftly moving water, he let out a whoosh of air. Until that moment, he hadn't even realized he'd been holding his breath.

As if her thoughts mirrored his, Jane came running up to him from her spot farther along the line of workers, who also appeared to be heaving a collective sigh of relief. "It's over," she said, shoving back the hood of her slicker. "Glory Ridge is safe." Her eyes were moist, her voice heavy with emotion.

He grinned down at her. "I think Dry Creek is a fraud. Seems it can get wet enough to make one hell of a nuisance of itself."

"Only once in a lifetime, I'm hoping."

Again he wanted to wrap his arms around her, and again he stopped himself, far from sure if she would welcome an audience. Because they would have one. Voices were buzzing around them. When the group let out a cheer, Adam pulled his gaze away from Jane long enough to see several people craning their necks, staring at the sky.

He looked up, too, and found a rainbow directly overhead. It was worthy of a cheer, he decided.

Then he looked down again and found her watching him. Just watching him.

And that was when he knew. That whispered declaration hadn't come from his imagination. Jane Pitt had told him she loved him, probably never expecting he would hear the words.

A part of him wanted to shout in triumph. But another more logical, reasonable part wasted little time in checking his enthusiasm. He was leaving in a matter of weeks, it reminded him. Because he didn't belong here.

As the crowd pulled Jane away to join in their high

spirits, Adam aimed a long look around him and saw
that the late-day sun was just setting, glazing the tops
of the towering pines bright orange. He'd gotten used
to that sight, he realized. Sunset was different here
than in the desert areas to the south. Sharper, somehow. Crisper. And sunrise was no slouch, either, for
all that he'd griped to himself more than once at the
prospect of getting up before dawn.

Adam's forehead knitted in a thoughtful frown.
He'd come to Glory Ridge seeking a closer relationship with his son, which was now a reality, thank
heaven. But maybe he'd gotten more than he'd bargained for. Far more. Maybe this peaceful place had
somehow snuck up on him and charmed him in a
way he'd never expected.

And maybe he could belong here...if he truly
wanted to.

Adam's frown deepened. Did he want to? he suddenly had to ask himself.

Damn right you do, something rising straight from
the core of him replied. *You care about this
place...and you care even more about its owner.
What would your future be like without her?*

Empty. That was how it would be, he abruptly
recognized. As much as he loved his son, he needed
more in his life. He needed the warm, caring woman
he'd come to know here. Without her, something
deep down inside him would always feel empty. Hollow.

The very same way he'd felt walking down the
endless corridor in that puzzling dream, opening
doors to find nothing behind them, searching for
something he could never quite make out. Until now.

This was the answer. *She* was the answer.

God, he not only cared about her, he—

"Hey, Dad!" Sam's sudden shout jarred Adam back to his surroundings. The boy jogged over to where his father stood, no longer wearing the slicker that had dwarfed him. Instead, the familiar shirt, a glaring mix of rockets and alien creatures, was on full display.

Sam skidded to a stop on the rain-slicked ground. "Everything's gonna be all right, huh?"

Adam knew it was a reference to the now-defeated waters. Nevertheless, his reply held a double meaning.

"Everything may wind up being a lot better than all right." He crouched down and dropped his voice to a level meant for Sam's ears alone. "When we get back to the cabin, I need to talk to you about something—about Jane…and other things."

Sam traded a man-to-man look with his father. "Are we gonna tell her we got lost?"

Hell, no, Adam thought, giving his head a swift shake. He and his male pride were never making that particular confession. No, he had a far different sort of conversation in mind. One that involved both his and his son's future. The discussion would be a serious one, but this wasn't the time for it.

"We'll talk later," he said, only to have his stomach underscore that statement with a loud groan of pure discontent.

In response, Sam grinned his boyish, lopsided grin. "Guess you're hungry."

"I am," Adam replied, although he hadn't even considered the possibility until that moment. What he was, he realized, was starving. And thirsty, as well, for something a lot more bracing than the bottled water that was all he'd had since dinner the evening before.

"I could drink a gallon of hot coffee," he said with feeling.

"We got coffee *and* food back at the office," Sam looked happy to report. "Sandwiches and potato salad and everything. Some ladies brought it. They said they were with some kinda women's awks-a-larry."

A smile tugged at Adam's lips. "I think you mean the Women's Auxiliary." He recalled that his mother had once belonged to that venerable organization.

"Uh-huh." Sam's grin was back. "They brought chocolate cake, too."

"Then let's get a piece," Adam told his son. "Or in your case, probably a second piece." Or maybe a third, he thought, but he wasn't worrying about a sugar overload today. "It's time to celebrate beating that storm at its own game."

He could only hope they'd have something else to celebrate, as well. And soon.

SHE GOT THE LAST PIECE of cake. Even the next day, as she logged the details of another new reservation into her ledger book, Jane could recall that it had tasted like a small slice of heaven. Now the crowd of well-wishers who hadn't hesitated to help in a crisis or share in her joy at its passing had long since departed. Today she was alone in the office.

And lonely, she had to admit. Not because the small room was no longer crammed with people, but because one particular person was missing.

"You've got to get used to not having him around," she lectured herself. "He'll be taking off for good in a couple of weeks." She closed the ledger with a snap and set it at one side of the desk. "Sure, you'll miss him, but you'll survive."

She had to. She had a job to do. And pining for one special man long after he was gone would serve no purpose—no purpose at all, her common sense told her.

She had to acknowledge the truth of that. Still, it didn't stop her from wishing she'd gotten at least a glimpse of him that day. Not that she didn't know where he was. Sam had poked his head in hours ago to tell her that he and his father were driving into town.

What she didn't know was what they planned on doing there.

"Going to Dewitt's for a hamburger and fries?" she'd asked, more to make conversation than anything.

But—somewhat oddly, she had to allow—Sam had neither confirmed nor denied it. He'd just stared at her for a second before saying, "Yeah, well, maybe." And with those hasty words, he'd turned and left her in the dust.

Jane leaned back in her creaky swivel chair and frowned up at the ceiling. Yes, *odd* would describe it, all right. The more she thought about it, the more certain she became on that score. The memory had her wondering if father and son just might be up to something, even if she had no idea what.

But since she had no idea, she'd probably be better off considering something else. She still had decisions to make before Glory Ridge Honeymoon Haven opened, including choosing some new outfits for its owner and hostess. She'd long since come to terms with the fact that she couldn't continue to wear what she wore today and had worn for too many years to count—well-washed shirt, battered jeans, scarred boots.

Adam had suggested cotton khakis for everyday wear, teamed with red polo shirts—to match the red trim around the little wooden hearts that held the names of the cabins. Jane resisted any thought of rolling her eyes. At least red wasn't pink. And what he'd proposed would probably be comfortable enough—not only for her but for the small staff she'd have to hire pretty quickly if business wound up being as good as her consultant seemed confident it would be.

"The man's been paid big bucks in the past because he has a history of getting it right," she reminded herself. "He's not likely to be wrong now." No, it was far more likely that Glory Ridge's new marketing strategy would turn out to be another feather in his cap.

Damage from yesterday's storm had been minimal, she'd discovered on an earlier inspection that morning. As much as it had hurt to see the old bridge over the creek go, it could be easily replaced, the construction crew had told her. And the creek itself was only a shadow of the swiftly moving river it had been. The weather pattern had already taken a welcome shift, and workers were hauling away the truckloads of sandbags.

The future looked promising, she couldn't deny, at least where the resort was concerned.

Once, just weeks ago, that would have been everything she could have asked for. Now things had changed and nothing would ever be quite the same—

although she was the only one who knew it, thank goodness.

Jane straightened in her seat at the sound of approaching footsteps. Seconds later Sam poked his head through the doorway, much as he had hours earlier. This time, he didn't hesitate to step into the office, swiftly followed by Adam.

The elder Lassiter had a brightly wrapped gift in hand, while the younger kept his small hands behind his back. Wearing an unreadable expression, Adam crossed the room with quiet steps and gave the beribboned box to Jane.

"What's this?" she asked.

He propped a denim-clad hip on a corner of the desk and folded his arms across his chest. "A birthday present."

Birthday? "You know my birthday's not until October."

"Early present," he amended. "I thought I'd follow your sister's example."

Because he wouldn't be here in October, Jane concluded. She refused to let that thought depress her. If she couldn't talk herself out of it, she'd have plenty of time to feel the pain of that loss after he was gone.

"Are you gonna open it?" Sam prompted, clearly eager for her to get on with the task.

So get on with it, she told herself. She set the gift in the center of the desk and tugged at the shiny yellow ribbon, loosening it enough to pull it off before she undid the blue and white striped paper. And then she couldn't help staring as she spotted the store logo scrawled across the center of the box.

Her gaze flew up to meet Adam's. "A *toy* store?"

He looked down at her, his bland expression still

revealing nothing. ''Why not? They have some terrific things there.''

''Yeah,'' Sam wasted no time in seconding. ''They got lots of good stuff.''

Jane raised an eyebrow. ''Don't you think I'm a little old for toys?'' she asked Adam. ''I gave mine up a long time ago.''

''You never had what's in there to give up,'' he replied with a short nod down at the box.

''Oh.'' Must be a new gadget of some kind. That's all Jane could figure out. Then she opened the box and discovered she couldn't have been more wrong.

It was a doll. A chubby-cheeked charmer with a riot of auburn curls, like the kind her sister had played with as a young child. Jane had never admitted to wanting one of her own—not even to Adam when the subject had come up one day.

''I didn't know if you'd like it,'' Sam confided, ''but my dad thought you would.''

''I do,'' she said quietly. What pleased her far more than the gift itself was the fact that Adam had not only remembered, but had obviously tried to make up for the lack of anything as frivolous as dolls in her childhood. Once upon a time, it would have secretly thrilled her, despite her tomboy image. Now, every time she saw it she would think of the man who'd given it to her.

The memory would make it even harder to watch him leave. Still, she couldn't be sorry, despite the fact that his thoughtfulness had her eyesight blurring. She hadn't shed any real tears since her great-aunt's death, and before that since she'd lost her mother long ago. But some would fall now, she knew, if she didn't get a handle on herself in a hurry.

"It wasn't supposed to make you sad," Sam said, sounding worried.

Jane dragged in a steadying breath and looked at the boy who'd been anything but happy to come to Glory Ridge. Although she'd liked him right from the start, she'd never expected back then to feel her heart twist at the prospect of never seeing him again. She'd miss him, she realized, every bit as much as she'd miss his father—although in a different way.

But she couldn't say so, of course. No, all she could do was reassure him.

"I'm not sad," she said, summoning the widest smile she could muster. "The doll just took me by surprise and I needed a minute to get my bearings." At least that was true enough, she thought.

"Okay." Sam appeared pleased to accept her at her word. He slid a questioning glance up at his father, seemed to find the answer he sought and again directed his attention to Jane. "We, uh, bought something else for you, too."

"Another birthday present?" she ventured.

"Not exactly," Sam hedged, shuffling his feet.

And what in the world did that mean? Jane asked herself. *Please,* she had to offer in a silent plea, *whatever it is, don't let me start bawling over it.*

After another brief hesitation, Sam produced a small, square box, one he'd kept hidden behind his back, and held it out to her. It wasn't from the toy store, she noted. Not unless toy stores had started packaging their wares in dark blue velvet.

Jewelry seemed the best bet. A pin, maybe. Or earrings. If it turned out to be the latter, she had to hope they weren't designed for pierced ears. Jane fought back a wince at the idea of anyone putting a needle through her earlobe.

But it wasn't earrings, or a pin, she soon discovered.

It was a ring. And not just any ring.

"Oh, my God," she whispered as the reality of what she was looking at finally sank in. It was the sort of ring a man gave a woman when he—

"We were wondering if you'd, uh, marry us," a young voice said haltingly.

Jane snapped her head up and stared at Sam as he continued, this time in a rush. "I mean we were wondering if you'd marry my dad. I'm not old enough to get married, and I don't like girls, anyway. But I like you," he assured her. "I like you a lot, even if you are a girl, 'cause you know how to catch a fish and do all kinds of cool things. And if you married my dad, we could all stay here."

Stay here. The words repeated in her mind as she slowly craned her neck back and met Adam's gaze. "You want to stay at Glory Ridge?"

His eyes never wavered from hers. "Yes."

She had to shake her head in an effort to clear her brain. "I don't understand," she said, meaning every word.

"I didn't, either," he told her, his tone turning as serious as she'd ever heard it. "Not until yesterday. I'm not saying it will be an easy transition, or that I won't miss some of the things I'm used to. Truth is, I'll probably keep the delivery people busy hauling in imported food and wine by the caseload. But this place means something to me. In fact, it means more to me than I ever realized until it nearly washed away." He paused. "I know I may never fit in as well as someone who's been raised in the great outdoors, but I want to be a part of it.''

Even though she saw the stark reality of that reflected in his gaze, she still had trouble believing he could be ready to turn his life upside down. ''What about your business?''

''It can be based here. I'll have to travel on occasion, but this would be home. I'd like to build a family-size cabin with an office to suit my needs, and spend my spare time helping my wife run her business…if you'll say yes.'' The beginnings of a smile curved his mouth. ''Since you already told me you loved me, I figured I at least had a chance.''

One more surprise, she thought. ''So you heard.''

''I did.''

Neither of them mentioned precisely when and under what very intimate circumstances he'd come by that knowledge. And neither would, Jane knew, with Sam all ears.

''So are you gonna say yes?'' Sam asked.

She studied the boy who'd touched her heart, then switched back to the man who now owned a big part of it. Was she going to say yes? she asked herself.

If you do, a niggling voice in the back of her mind said, *can you be sure he won't turn his back on you someday in favor of a prettier and more sophisticated woman?*

In response, she couldn't help remembering the stinging rejection she'd once suffered at another man's hands. But if she let that stop her, the future would be lost. She had to trust *this* man to keep her heart safe. And all at once she did.

''I guess I will say yes,'' she conceded at last, ''provided I hear the magic words.''

Sam blinked. "Huh? What are the magic words, Dad?"

Adam stared straight into Jane's eyes. "I love you," he told her. Then, leaning down, he took the jeweler's box from her, plucked out the ring, with its sparkling diamond, and placed it on her finger. "There's no getting rid of us now," he warned, his large hand closing over hers. "The ring fits, thank God, and Sam and I are here to stay."

"Yippee!" Sam jumped up and down. "Can I call Travis and tell him?"

"I don't see why not," Jane said at Adam's questioning lift of a brow. "The news will get around soon enough."

"Undoubtedly," he acknowledged. "There will probably be a bridal shower in your future."

A shower. She'd had to be dragged to the few she'd attended in the past. Way too much muss and fuss, as far as she was concerned, plus all that ribbing of the bride-to-be. "I must love you a lot to let myself in for one of those."

Adam's eyes took on a gleam as he pulled his cell phone from his belt and handed it to Sam. "How about making that call outside? Jane and I have some unfinished business here."

Sam made a face. "I guess you're gonna kiss her, huh?"

"Absolutely."

Jane jotted the Malloy number on a piece of scratch paper and gave it to Sam. "I want a big hug later," she told him.

"If I gotta, I gotta," he said, heaving a gusty sigh. But he was grinning as he ran from the room.

Jane had to grin herself. "That is one great kid."

"You bet," the proud father agreed. "And I'd like to have some more."

"Hmm. I don't know anything about babies," she reminded him, although the thought of having Adam's child sent a shiver of anticipation through her. "I never even played with dolls."

"Luckily, I have plenty of hands-on experience," he assured her as he drew her to her feet and tugged her into his arms. "I'll take my hug now."

He had his hug, plus a lengthy kiss that threatened to melt her bones. Finally, he let her up for air, but he didn't let her go. Instead, he kept her close and slid his long fingers into the threadbare rear pockets of her jeans.

"You might give a person fair notice when you're going to propose," Jane told him. "I would've gotten a little spruced up for the occasion."

He pressed her closer still. "Not that I plan on complaining whenever you want to drive me crazy with a sexy nightgown, but you do a damn fine job of it in ancient jeans, too."

She reached up a hand and brushed it through his hair. "Oh, yeah?"

"Yeah. You're all woman. My woman. And just for the record," he added, locking his gaze with hers, "I think you're the most beautiful thing that ever happened to me."

Her heart not only fluttered at those words. It soared.

Then he was kissing her again, slowly and tenderly this time. Kissing him back, Jane didn't hesitate to pour everything she had into it, every bit of her love for him and all of her hopes and dreams for the future.

Suddenly, that future was looking downright wonderful, she thought.

She might have fallen hook, line and sinker for a fancy man, but she'd also landed herself a handsome husband. He'd make a tall, dark and gorgeous groom, no doubt about it.

And she knew the perfect spot for a honeymoon.

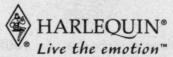

If you enjoyed what you just read,
then we've got an offer you can't resist!

Take 2 bestselling
love stories FREE!
Plus get a FREE surprise gift!

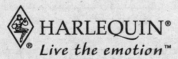

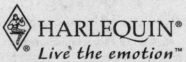